Cum for Me 7
Jack Be Nimble,
Jack Be Quick

Sugar E. Wallz

**Lock Down Publications &
Ca$h Whispers**
Cum for Me 7

Cum for Me 7

Lock Down Publications
Po Box 944
Stockbridge, Ga 30281

Visit our website at **www.lockdownpublications.com**

First Edition May 2021
Printed in the United States of America
*This is a work of fiction. Names, characters, places, and
incidents either are products of the author's imagination
or are used fictitiously. Any similarity to actual events or
locales or persons, living or dead, is entirely coinci-
dental.*
Cover design and layout by: Dynasty's Cover Me
Book interior design by: Shawn Walker
Edited by: Tamira Butler

Stay Connected with Us!

Text **LOCKDOWN** to 22828 to stay up-to-date with new releases, sneak peaks, contests and more...

Thank you!

Submission Guideline.

Submit the first three chapters of your completed manuscript to ldpsubmissions@gmail.com, subject line: Your book's title. The manuscript must be in a .doc file and sent as an attachment. Document should be in Times New Roman, double spaced and in size 12 font. Also, provide your synopsis and full contact information. If sending multiple submissions, they must each be in a separate email.

Have a story but no way to send it electronically? You can still submit to LDP/Ca$h Presents. Send in the first three chapters, written or typed, of your completed manuscript to:

LDP: Submissions Dept
Po Box 944
Stockbridge, Ga 30281

DO NOT send original manuscript. Must be a duplicate.

Provide your synopsis and a cover letter containing your full contact information.

Thanks for considering LDP and Ca$h Presents.

Caution: This book contains explicit content and may cause sudden arousal.

This book is dedicated to the only man who makes me wet.

My husband, my soulmate,

Robert "Twelve" Foster Jr.

Your name alone makes me cum.

Aaah!!!

I.

I like to fuck.

That's it and that's all.

There is no greater feeling than cumming, and I try to do it each and every day.

Hey, a good nut never hurt nobody.

Right?

So, why don't you "cum" into my world and experience what a good fuck really is. I promise you'll never want to leave.

And if you're not already naked, don't worry, you will be.

II.

Jack be nimble, Jack be quick,
My pussy stays wet inside.
A sense of euphoria comes over me,
And it's not something I try to hide.
Male, female, dick, or tongue,
Either one will do just fine.
And even when I'm all alone,
I'll play in this pussy of mine.
Jack be nimble, Jack be quick,
It just would not seem right,
If I didn't answer my body's calling,
And get fucked every night.
With one partner, maybe even two,
I'm always wanting more.
I just wanna be fucked so right,
Daddy leave this pussy sore.
Jack be nimble, Jack be quick,
You can use one finger or five.
It doesn't really matter to me,
But I need to cum and stay alive,
So welcome to my life,
You can stay as long as you please.
Go ahead and pull it out,
I'm already on my knees.
Breakfast, lunch, and dinner,
Just stuff me with some dick.
Yeah, you can also stay for dessert,
But Jack be nimble, Jack be quick.

Sugar E. Wallz

Chapter One

I could feel the wetness before I even opened my eyes. My clit was pulsing and felt as if it had its own heartbeat, and who knows, maybe it did. I knew that there was no way I could get out of bed until I did what needed to be done. So, I slid my panties down and spread my pussy open. This had become routine for me, and it seemed like in order to start my day, I needed to cum first. Cumming was like my cup of coffee, and it definitely woke me up.

As I began massaging my clit with small circular motions, a moan escaped from deep within. "Mmm." This shit felt so good, but I knew it wouldn't be enough to satisfy my sexual appetite, so I reached over to my nightstand and pulled the one drawer open, and there it was. I got a little more excited once I had the eight-inch black dildo in my small hand. Although it wasn't real, I always imagined it was attached to a dark chocolate, rugged looking thug. I brought it to my lips and sucked the head of it into my mouth like it could really feel the warmth of my saliva coating it. I sucked on it for a few more minutes and tugged on my clit with my thumb and forefinger at the same time, bringing me even more pleasure.

I needed to be fucked so bad, and after I wet the dildo with my saliva, I put it down between my thighs and slowly inserted it into my waiting pussy. I pushed it in and pulled it out really slow, as I imagined a thug tearing my pussy up. I began to speed up and fuck myself harder, imagining he was punishing me for being a bad girl. Long, slow strokes and then deep, hard ones. "Oh yes, ssss," I moaned, since I didn't know whose name to call. All I knew was that it felt so good I had to call somebody. So, I called my own name. "Yeah, Nikki, fuck this pussy."

In and out slowly, and then pull it all the way out and rub it on my clit. Then, in and out faster while my fingers press on my clit. I wanted to put myself in a better position so I could fuck myself harder, so I got on my knees and positioned the dildo under me. I then slid down on it, taking it all the way in and trying to hit all of my walls. "Oh shit, yeah. This is so good." I talked and moaned louder with each passing second. I rode the dildo as if it was a real dick, giving myself insurmountable pleasure. I began to get chills and felt my knees get weak. I knew then that I was about to cum. "Ooh, ooh, yeah." I could feel the pressure leaving me as my cum began squirting out all over the big black dick inside of me. "Yes, fuck yes."

As I continued to cum, I didn't let up. I could feel my whole body shaking and making me submit to the hand-held dick that I possessed. I stayed on it until I knew that nothing else was coming out of me. After I finished cumming, I pulled the dildo out slowly and began sucking all of my juices off of it. I loved the taste of my pussy, and since I couldn't actually put my lips on it, I had to improvise and taste it the best way I could. My pussy tasted so sweet and so good, I'm sure I could have bottled up its juices and sold it. As good as it was, I would have been a millionaire. When I was done with my session, I noticed the time and knew I needed to get up and get ready for work. I wiped off my toy with Handi Wipes and placed it back in the drawer. I then got up and went and hopped in the shower, and planned what I was going to do that day. It was something I had been wanting to do for a long time but never had the courage to do. However, today would be the day I would pull through. I was smiling the entire time I soaped up. When I got out of the shower, I dried off, got dressed, and took one last look in the mirror before leaving out the door.

Chapter Two

I came to work today with no panties on. I needed to be ready when it was time to handle my business. I didn't need anything standing in my way. I had been wanting to fuck Jamal for the longest. Jamal just so happened to be my boss, and I could tell from the print in his slacks that his dick was ginormous. So what? He's married, but I really don't give a fuck. All I knew was that I wanted that dark chocolate dick deep inside of me. Mmm, mmm, mmm, just thinking about it had me sitting here with a wet pussy.

"Nicole, I need those reports today." I almost jumped out of my skin when I heard his voice. My clit pulsed every time he spoke to me. I wasn't sure if there was ever another man I wanted this bad. I loved dick and on occasion, I loved pussy too, but for some reason, I would not be content until I had the dick that was attached to the man in front of me. At that moment, he was the only one who could curb my sexual desires.

As I put together the papers of the report for him, I could feel the stickiness between my legs. I vowed to myself that I would not walk out of his office today until he fucked me. I gathered the papers in my arm and walked straight into his office. I usually knocked, but today was not a day for formalities. As soon as I walked in, I began unbuttoning my blouse. "Good, I hope…" those were all the words Jamal got out before he noticed my nipple poking through my sheer bra.

"You hope what, Mr. Jackson?" I asked as I popped the snap on the front of my bra and released my breasts from their prison.

Jamal just sat there with a loss for words, so I decided to give him a little show to start this thing off right. My nipples were begging to be sucked, so I pushed one of my breasts up to my mouth and stuck my tongue out, and began to lick around my erect nipple. As I flicked my tongue over it, I pulled and pinched on the other one with my other hand. Jamal was stuck and seemed to not know how to respond. I kept eye contact with him as I began walking toward him.

The closer I got to him, the more I could see his dick harden. When I got directly in front of him, I let my skirt drop to the floor. "I, I can't..." I put my finger to his lips to shush him, because I wasn't trying to hear no bullshit.

I pushed all of his papers off his desk and then sat down in front of him. I could see him sweating, and his nervousness made me wetter. There was a certain kind of rush you get when you are fucking and scared of getting caught. "We can't ..."

I lifted my right leg and put my foot on his chest, pushing him back in the chair. "Yes, we can," I told him before pulling my other leg up, and then I rested both of my feet on his thighs. I knew he could see the juices coming out of my pussy, causing it to have a glistening effect.

He tried to speak again, "Nicole, I-I'm-I'm married." I smiled and acted like I didn't hear him, and then spread my legs further, revealing my shaved pussy.

My clit poked out from between my lips and was begging to be touched, so I happily obliged and said, "Don't be scared of this pussy, Mr. Jackson." I then let out a little chuckle and continued, "Trust me, it's well worth it." All I had my mind on was getting fucked, and one way or another, his dick was going inside of this pussy today.

I began to massage my swollen clit while looking Jamal in the eyes. I winked at him and said seductively, "Suck it, Jamal. Suck my pussy." That nigga's wife became a distant memory as he sucked my clit into his mouth. "Yes, Jamal. Yes. That's what I'm talking about." I proceeded to talk shit to him as he sucked me harder. "This pussy tastes good, don't it, Jamal?" All of a sudden, I felt two of his fingers slide into my pussy really slow. "Oh shit, Jamal, you gonna make me cum. Yes."

I grabbed the back of his head and began to push on it, giving him no space to move, and then tightened my thighs, holding him in place. I wanted to cum all over his face and wanted to make sure nothing was wasted. "Yes, Jamal. Make this pussy cum." He then started sucking harder and flicking his tongue over it at the same time. My moans became louder. "Mmm, mmm." Jamal was sucking

14

on my clit like it was the only thing keeping him alive. I couldn't hold it any longer. "I'm cumming, Jamal. Don't stop. I'm fucking cumming. Aaah." As my juices began to squirt out of me, he continued to suck, making me weaker by the second. When I was done cumming, he licked my pussy hole, making sure he left nothing behind.

I was hoping this nigga's dick worked good as his tongue, because his head game was damn sure on point. Before I fucked him, I wanted to taste him, so I pushed him all the way back in his chair again and dropped down to my knees. As I was undoing his pants, he demanded, "You better suck this dick right. Got me cheating on my wife and shit."

His dick was so hard that when I pulled his pants down, it slapped me in the face. I laid my eyes on the nicest, fattest dick I'd ever seen, and said, "Oh, I'm about to swallow this dick."

I smiled and began to lick around the head, making sure to get the pre-cum coming out of the little hole. I then pulled the whole head into my mouth and sucked gently while running my hand up and down his shaft. When Jamal opened his mouth and said, "That's the best you got?" I made his dick completely disappear. As I pushed his dick deep into my mouth, I began caressing his balls and heard a moan escape from his pussy-drenched lips. "Oh yeah, mmm hmm."

Jamal slid further down in his chair, and as I sucked the head of his dick, I started flicking my tongue over it at the same time, and then I'd go all the way down to the base. I could have sworn that I saw that nigga's toes curl up through his shoes, as I heard him say to me, "Yeah, just like that. You 'bout to make me cum."

I suddenly began to feel his vein pulsating, but this nigga had me fucked up if he thought he was going to cum before he fucked me, hell no. I wasn't through with him yet, so I let the dick fall out of my mouth. I could tell by his look that he wondered what I was doing. "Nah, Jamal, I'ma need you to fuck me before I swallow them seeds." I knew that if I'd let him cum before fucking me, he would be done, and that was not about to happen. "I came into this office today to fuck, and I'm not leaving until it's done," I said to him while looking in his eyes. I then got up off my knees, turned my back to him, leaned over the desk, and spread my ass cheeks. "Fuck me, Jamal."

He then got up out of his chair, and as he positioned himself behind me, he said, "Don't worry, this pussy is about to get fucked." I could tell by how hard he gripped my hips that he was going to be very aggressive, and that shit made my heart skip a beat. I usually liked being in control of things, but being dominated by him at that very moment sent me over the edge.

As he pushed the head of his dick into me, opening me up, I felt his thumb enter my asshole. I caught an instant rush that I was not expecting. Jamal suddenly fell into a whole new role. "You want me to fuck you, bitch?" When he asked me that, it turned me on even more.

"Yes, Jamal, fuck this pussy. Yes." And that's exactly what he did. He rammed his beautiful rod up inside of me so hard, I almost lost my breath. As he was hitting me from the back, his balls were slamming into my clit, giving me extra pleasure. "Oh yes, fuck me just like that." Jamal was continually pushing his thumb in my ass the entire time he was fucking me, and I was on the brink of another orgasm. "Fuck me harder, Jamal. Fuck this pussy harder." It felt like his dick was getting bigger with every stroke. I wondered if he fucked his wife with such intensity and aggression, or was he teaching me a lesson for being the one who made him cheat.

I could feel his dick beginning to pulse and knew that he was about to cum. "Bitch, I'm about to cum." He said it angrily and didn't let up at all. I wanted to taste his juices and pushed him back really hard so he would fall out of me, and then I instantly turned around and pulled his dick into my mouth, sucking with extra force. "Yeah, suck that dick." As he began cumming, he said, "Swallow all of it. Yes."

The taste of his cum mixed with mine was like an exotic fruit that was hard to find, so hard that you had to go to other countries just to get it. After I emptied him, I let his dick go and looked up at him. No words needed to be exchanged, because we both knew that we would do this again. As we finished getting dressed, we heard a knock at the door, and then Terry walked in. Jamal's wife.

I wondered how long she had been outside the door before finally knocking; however, I wasn't going to stick around and see what happened with them, because I really didn't give a fuck. I got what I came for. Shit, next time, I'm gonna ask him to invite his bitch, because a little pussy never hurt anybody.

Chapter Three

It had been a couple of days since my tryst with Jamal, but it felt kind of awkward around the office. I wanted to ask him if his wife knew what we had done, but fuck him, because their happy home didn't mean shit to me. The weekend was here and I was ready to turn up. Since it was Friday, I decided I would go out and enjoy myself. Hell, I deserved it after working all week. I didn't have many female friends because they just didn't understand me. The ones I did have usually kept their distance from me. They would get offended when they would ask my opinion on something. I was always taught to be honest, so if their outfit was ugly, I would be the bitch to tell them. If they didn't want to know, then they shouldn't have asked. With that fact in mind, I would be going out solo, as always.

I took off my work clothes and prepared myself for a nice hot shower. As the water flowed out, it hit my nipples and my adrenaline spiked. I flinched a little at the sensation. I stayed horny, so it took very little to excite me. I discovered my cravings for orgasms at the young age of fourteen. I just happened to be bathing and when I opened my pussy to wash it, I must have hit my clit just right because I got instant chills. However, I didn't react to that feeling until later on that night when I was in bed. I first thought I was tripping, but when I put my finger on my clit and pressed down hard, I felt those same chills and the rest was history.

My mama must have heard me moaning through the thin walls in our house, because she used to tell me, "Nicole, your little young ass sounds like you're possessed with a sex demon." She would spend many nights praying over me while I pretended to be asleep, but as soon as she walked out of my room, I would pull my panties to the side and stroke that little man in the boat until he drowned. It would take much more than prayers to curb my sexual desires.

I was trying to ignore the feeling that the warm shower water was giving me, but who was I to ignore something so obvious? I pinched my nipples with my thumb and forefinger and pulled on them lightly. I imagined someone's mouth on them, teasing them with their tongue. "Mmm, yes." An instant moan escaped from within me as I pinched and pulled harder. "Oh god, yes." I reached up to the shower head and changed it to jet stream, and the force of the water made me lose my breath. I propped a leg up on the side of the shower edge, and as my pussy opened up freely, I let the water molest my clit. The water was so hard and forceful that all I had to do was stand there. I continued playing with my nipples while allowing the water to handle the rest.

I began thinking of Jamal's big dick and all the things I wanted to do to him the next time I got the chance. I wished that I would have brought my toy in here with me, but I was not about to interrupt this feeling to go get it. As I felt myself about to cum, I moved my leg from the ledge. I wanted to try something different, so I turned around and bent over. As I spread my ass cheeks open, the water began to hit my pussy full force, so I reached down between my legs and began stroking my clit. "Ssss." The force of my finger and the water combined caused me to cum so hard I almost fell over. "Oh, shit. Yes, yes." I was so loud I'm sure my neighbors could hear me. That shit felt amazing, but like all good things, it must come to an end. After that awesome orgasm, I finished with my shower and then got out. It was time to prepare myself for the night ahead.

Chapter Four

I wanted to be extra sexy for tonight because I was going to one of the hottest strip clubs in town. The club was called "Poppers" and the name alone should have told you why. Them hoes popped their pussies and asses in ways that would make your back cringe, but it was sexy as fuck. This would be my second time going and I was determined to make this visit count.

I pulled up in my Lexus and noticed all types of men standing around waiting to look at some pussy. I also noticed some females preparing themselves for a night of entertainment, but they weren't much to look at. When women came to places like this, it was usually to pick up guys. They knew the men would be horny after watching the dancers and would be looking for a hookup afterwards. For these women, coming to a place like this was the only action they got.

When I stepped out of my ride, all eyes were on me, but who could blame them? I had on a low-cut Fendi tank and a pair of white Fendi jeans that formed to my ass and thighs just right. I wore a pair of open-toe, strappy heels to match and had my hair pulled up into a messy bun. My tank was just high enough to show off my flat stomach and diamond belly ring. My whole being screamed "I wanna fuck," and that's exactly what I wanted it to do.

"What's up lil' mama?" The voice alone paralyzed me, and when I looked up at him, I wanted to surrender and let him fuck me right then and there. I didn't care that the parking lot was packed with other people and didn't mind putting on a show for them. This nigga had shoulder-length dreads with hazel eyes. His six-foot frame and dark skin complemented the white polo shirt he had on. However, I couldn't let him distract me from my mission. When he spoke, my body trembled. "You need some company tonight?"

My mind screamed yes, but my body was craving something else, and he wasn't ready for the response I gave him, "Nah, daddy. Tonight, I'm trying to suck on some pussy. But who knows what tomorrow will bring?" He just stood there in shock and didn't know how to react, so I turned around and walked away. I was looking for something different tonight. A flavor I hadn't tasted in a while. The flavor of some good pussy.

When I got to the entrance, the line began to part so that I could go right in, and that had me feeling like a VIP. I didn't protest at all as I sashayed my ass past the crowd. Once I went inside, I made my way to the cash counter so I could change my bills into singles. I wanted a nice stack to throw on stage to the dancers. I could feel the many eyes in the building staring at me, and it only made me switch harder as I walked away.

I got a table up front so I could be closer to the pussy popping in my face. I wanted to be able to inhale the aroma of the pussy, which would make it easier for me to pick who was sharing my bed with me tonight. I sat there for a while, watching all of the dancers, and although they turned me on, they didn't give me the feeling I was longing for. Since I didn't find what I wanted, I decided I would leave and go somewhere else. As I rose from my seat, that's when I saw her. They introduced her as Remy, and I could see why. Her skin looked to be as smooth as the finest wine, and I bet her pussy would make me tipsy.

As she removed her top, we made eye contact. I licked my lips and wondered what her perky nipples would feel like between them. As she put her fingers around them and began twisting and pulling, she gave me a wink and smiled. She then began grinding her pussy against the pole, and I envisioned it being on my face with her clit under the wetness of my tongue. I imagined I could hear her calling my name while rotating her hips to the pressure of my fingers inside of her. I could tell she felt my energy from the look in her eyes, and didn't waste any time peeling off bills to throw on stage for her. Instead, I threw the whole wad of cash that I had left as I walked all the way up to the stage. I couldn't help myself, I had to have a closer look.

She smiled as she began to walk closer to the edge of the stage where I was. She didn't say anything as she kneeled down, spread her legs, and pulled her thong to the side, revealing the prettiest pussy I had ever seen. I could see her juices glistening in the folds of her essence and wished that I could put my mouth on it right then.

As Remy began grinding her hips to the beat of the music, I felt a rush go through me, and as she stuck her tongue out and licked her top lip, I came.

I could feel a sense of loss when her set was over and she left the stage. I decided to sit back down and wait, hoping her presence would grace the stage again. Time passed slowly and Remy never came back. I felt a little disappointment and figured that I should leave. As soon as I got up from my chair, she appeared. "What's your name? You look bored. Maybe I can entertain you."

Her voice was melodic and as sexy as she was. It was causing me to move in slow motion as I responded to her. "I'm Nikki, and yeah, I am bored. What you gonna do to fix that?"

She smiled and replied, "Let's take a ride and I'll show you." That's all she had to say, and we were on our way out the door. I could feel everyone around us standing back and watching, wishing they were walking out with us, but I wasn't sharing this pussy tonight. I was hungry, and I needed to eat the entire plate to get full.

She had on a short skirt with no panties on. Her ass was poking out, begging for me to touch it, so I happily obliged. I could see the onlookers drooling, so I made sure to lift the skirt up enough to see her bare ass under the grip of my hand. When we got to my car, I walked her to the passenger side and opened the door for her. She slid into the seat, slowly putting in one leg at a time, exposing her pretty, plump pussy lips. I wanted to get on my knees right then and there but decided I should wait, although my adrenaline was in overdrive. Once she was all the way in, I closed the door and walked around to the driver side. I was hoping I could maintain until we got to my place, but the bitch was making it hard to do.

By the time I got into the car and shut the door, she had turned her back to the passenger side door and her pussy to me. She giggled and said hungrily, "Don't mind me, I'm just getting comfortable." She had her legs wide open with one propped on the dashboard and the other propped up on the back of the driver's seat. The bitch was bold, and all I could do was shake my head because I knew that I was about to have the time of my life. When I started the car and pulled off in traffic, all I could think about were the many ways I was going to fuck Remy tonight. I wondered if Remy was her real name or just a stage name but brushed the thought to the side, because honestly, I didn't give a fuck. I wasn't trying to start a relationship. I just wanted to fuck, so her name didn't mean shit.

While driving down the highway, I happened to glance over and saw Remy playing with her pussy. I was trying to be cool about it, but her moaning was making it hard for me to keep my eyes on the road. "Oh yeah. Mmm."

I didn't say anything to her but while she played with her clit, I reached over and pushed two fingers into her. "Damn, this pussy is wet," I said to her in an excited tone.

She replied, "Yeah, boo, this fat pussy stays wet." I finger fucked her nice and slow but had plans later on to fuck her nice and hard. Her moans took me to a whole different level. "Uh, mmm, mmm." I couldn't wait to tear this pussy up, and the thought of it made me drive faster.

Remy was grinding on my fingers like they were a big dick lodged up inside of her, and it felt so damn good. It was at that time that I wished I'd worn something loose so that she could play in my pussy too. Just thinking about it had me soaking wet. "Oh yeah, I'm about to cum." And with that said, she began squirting her juices out all over my fingers.

After she came, I pulled both fingers out and put one in her mouth. "Suck that shit, baby," I told her as she cleaned her cum off of me. I saved the other finger for me and when she was done, I put the other one in my mouth and sucked her cum down my throat.

I was in a zone when she said, "I got a whole lot more where that came from."

I looked at her and replied, "Oh yeah? Well, it just so happens that I'm dehydrated and really thirsty." I began to think that maybe I should have brought the chocolate dread with us, because I bet she could suck a mean dick. The thought of one going down her throat was a sweet vision, but it quickly left my mind because I knew that I didn't want to share this pussy with anyone.

When we walked into my condo, Remy walked over to my sound system and put on a Keith Sweat album. "Uh uh," I said, and went right behind her and changed it to some Plies, because I wasn't there to make love. I was trying to fuck. Hell, if she acted right, I might just call her my bust it baby.

When I turned back around, Remy was lying back on my sofa, butt ass naked with her fat pussy on full display. She looked at me devilishly and demanded, "Come over here and taste this pussy."

Who was I to argue? I responded as I walked over to her and got on my knees in front of her, "Bitch, this pussy ain't ready for me."

The look in her eyes was seductive yet innocent. I shoved a finger into her open hole and began going in and out of her. Her pussy was so wet it was like a pipe had burst inside of her. "Yes. Yes."

As her wetness coated my finger, I used my other hand to attack her clit. It was hard and begging for me to suck, but I wanted to play with it for a little while first. While playing in her pussy, I imagined a big dick going in and out of her and told myself that after I sucked this pussy, I would get the big boy out of the nightstand and give her the ride of her life. Her moans and shit talking were driving me crazy. "Yes, Nikki, fuck me. It feels so damn good." She paused and then continued, "Fuck this pussy and make it cum."

I was moving my fingers in and out of her faster and harder and was getting hungrier by the second. I finally bent down and pulled her swollen clit into my mouth. I acted like her clit was an oxygen tube and without it I would stop breathing, so I sucked it even harder. "Oh, fuck. You 'bout to make me cum, Nikki." I continued finger fucking her at the same time. "Suck it, baby. Suck that shit harder." Remy was working her hips while pounding her pussy into my face so hard I thought I would be bruised by the time I was done. However, I couldn't stop. I wanted to suck her pussy dry. "I'm cumming, oh my god. I'm cumming." Remy's juices started coating my fingers and I still didn't let up. When I started sucking on her clit even harder, she tried to pull away from me, but the arm of the couch had her stuck.

I finally released her from my grip and was licking her cum up off of her. She came so hard that it was dripping down to her asshole, so I licked that clean too. Remy had some good pussy, and I wasn't even getting started good yet. I planned on sucking and fucking her all night in all types of positions. My thong was soaking wet, and when I started getting undressed and went to pull them down, they stuck to my skin. She sat up on the couch and acted like she couldn't wait. She pulled me to her, and my knees buckled as she pulled my swollen bud into her mouth. "Ssss." That's all I could get out as she pulled my right leg up and rested it on the couch beside her. She then let my clit go and took her fingers and pulled the hood back on my clit, exposing it completely. "Fuck." That shit gave me a rush as she flicked her tongue over it hard and fast.

I reached over and grabbed her hair forcefully while pulling her deeper into my pussy. I fucked her mouth like I was punishing her for being so damn good at this shit. I used my free hand to pull and twist my nipples one at a time. "Suck this pussy, Remy. Bitch, I'm about to cum." She started sucking on my clit harder while flicking her tongue over it at the same time. She had me feeling like I had just inhaled the strongest drug known to man, and I couldn't hold it in any longer.

Remy didn't miss a beat as my cum started squirting out all over her chin. It was the hardest orgasm I'd had in a long time, and one that was desperately needed. She continued to move her head to the rhythm of my hips until I fell into her. When I finished cumming, I bent over and pulled her into a kiss. The taste of my cum made me ready for round two. I stood back up and grabbed her hand, pulling her from the sofa. "Come on. I got something special for you." It was time to take her into the bedroom where a very long night awaited us.

Chapter Five

On the way to the bedroom, I walked behind her so I could watch her ass jiggle. I was so mesmerized by her that I almost tripped over my own two feet. When we made it to the bedroom, I told Remy to lie down and get herself ready for what I had in store for her, but instead, she got on all fours and arched her back with her ass up in the air. Damn. This bitch was a straight freak and made me consider keeping her around for a while. That thought didn't stay long, because although I liked her a lot, this bitch was only here for one night and then she had to go.

I walked up behind her and spread her ass cheeks, looking at the vision in front of me. When I bent down and started licking her ass, she flinched and said, "Oh shit, that feels good." After licking around her asshole, I went down to her pussy and stuck my long, pointed tongue in the hole and at the same time, I reached my hand up and pulled on her clit. Being the type of woman I am, I knew that I had the abilities to make her cum back to back, but I wasn't ready for Remy to cum again, so I flipped her over on her back and lay on top of her.

We started grinding on each other and then got in the scissors position so our clits could touch. "Come on, Remy. Give me this pussy." I grinded as hard as my hips would let me, and the pressure was slowly building. I was about to cum and wanted Remy to cum with me. "Cum with me, Remy." As we came together, we kept grinding on each other. It was slippery from our juices and caused us both to giggle. I then rolled over and lay down on my back, getting my mind together so I could be ready for the next round. It always amazed me how high my sex drive was, and I figured that was why I didn't want to settle down. I didn't think there was anyone in this world who could keep up with my sexual needs. Hell, I was the type of bitch who could drain porn star dicks with my untamable hunger.

I had my eyes closed when I felt something brush against my cheek. I opened my eyes up and noticed Remy brushing my cheek with her fingertips. "Uh uh," I said while pulling my face away, and then continued, "I don't know what you thinking or what the fuck you doing, but I'm not on no romantic bullshit, Remy."

She pulled her hand back and said in a sassy, pissed off tone, "Fine. I'm sorry." Her attitude didn't last long, and she smiled seductively and asked, "Would you rather me do this instead?" She then started rolling her nipples between her fingers, which caused me to perk up.

"Now that's what the fuck I'm talking about. Do that shit." I smiled and just watched, because I didn't want to mess up her flow. I really just wanted to watch her enjoy what she had going on. When she started to get up, I stopped her and said, "Give me a good show, Remy." I already knew that she wouldn't disappoint me. I leaned back against the headboard and got comfortable. She was a beautiful sight to look at, and her smooth, tanned skin made her dark nipples stand out even more. Remy might have stripped for a living but at the end of the day, this freak was a lady. It's a shame all I had to offer her was a good fuck.

I licked my lips as she continued rolling her nipples between her fingers. She then stuck out her long tongue and flicked it over each nipple while looking me dead in the eyes, "Yes, Remy. Yes." Me saying that must have given her a little more motivation, because she then got up on her knees and straddled my legs. She moved a hand from her nipples and reached down between her thighs, spreading her pussy lips. Her clit was poking out, looking as if it was about to bust open. I wanted to reach out and touch it but maintained, because I was liking her groove. I wanted to see her cum, so I told her, "Make that pussy cum for me." I wanted to see that pussy juice coat her fingers before I rejoined the party.

While massaging her clit, she began to rotate her hips to the rhythm. "Ah, yes," she said, making it even harder for me to lay back and do nothing.

My pussy was sopping wet and only getting wetter by the second. I had held on for as long as I could, and stated, "It's time for me to give you what you really want."

I sat up and pulled one of her perky nipples into my mouth and began flicking my tongue over it really fast while sucking it at the same time. I reached down and stroked her engorged clit with my fingers. Squeezing it and pulling on it. "Lay down and let me fuck you the right way," I told her hungrily.

Remy smiled that big smile of hers and did as I said. She then replied, "Well, it's about time." She giggled as she lay back. As I spread her legs apart, I could see her wet hole waiting to be opened by the big black toy I was now holding. She and I both knew that I was about to tear this pussy up like I was a real man deep inside of her. I didn't have to put it in my mouth to wet it because her pussy was wet enough to allow it to slide right in.

As I leaned down to suck her clit into my mouth, I said, "I hope you are ready for this."

She replied, "Fuck yeah," as I pulled it between my lips and then slowly slid the dildo right in. I pulled it out and only let the head of it stay in for a minute. "Oh shit, Nicole. That feels so good, but I'm gonna need you to do better than that."

That comment made me feel like she was calling my fuck game whack, so I was about to make her pay for that. I rammed the whole dildo into her really hard, as if it had a grudge against her. I showed her no mercy as I pulled it in and out, fucking her harder with each stroke. I was gonna teach her ass what to say out of her mouth.

"You like this dick, Remy?" It was my turn to talk shit. "This enough dick for you now?" I fucked her hard and then slowly pushed a finger in her ass.

"Yes, Nikki. Yes, fuck me. Shit." I knew she felt this pressure all the way in her chest. She wasn't talking shit about doing better now.

"This what you wanted?"

"Yes. Yes."

I pushed it in one good time, and her cum started squirting out all over the dick in my hand. "Cum for me, girl. Cum for me."

I pulled the dick out and then pushed the head of it into her ass until she begged me to stop. "Oh my god. I can't take it anymore." I began to ease up as her cum drained from out of her. When I pulled the dildo out, I ran my tongue over her hole, licking up the juices around it. "Oh shit. That was so good."

I just smiled because I knew I had done my part. I grabbed her hand and pulled her from the bed so we could go rinse off and then get some much-needed rest.

I slept for hours, and when I finally woke, I looked over and Remy was gone. All she left behind was her scent and a short note that read, "Can't wait to see you again." Underneath those words were her phone number and a lipstick kiss. I smiled at the gesture. I couldn't wait to see her again either. It had been a long time since I had that much fun, and I knew that next time it would be a little more interesting, because I was going to make sure I brought us some company.

Chapter Six

Monday morning came without warning, and it felt like the weekend never existed. As I got ready for my day at the office, I hoped that the awkwardness with Jamal would disappear as soon as I walked in. I really wanted to ask him what his fucking problem was. Hell, that nigga should be happy because good pussy was hard to come by, and I gave him the best. He should have been walking around with his head held high after running up in this.

I decided to wear a sheer wrap-around skirt that accentuated my assets and, of course, no panties. My sleeveless top stuck to my breasts like a second skin, and no bra was needed. I didn't have any intentions on fucking Jamal today, but I wanted him to notice me even more than before. There was a lot of tension between us, and I wanted to break it so things could be comfortable again.

I noticed on my way to work that my gas hand was close to empty and figured I'd better stop and take care of it. When I pulled up to full serve, the attendant walked up to my ride to see how much I wished to purchase. As I was getting out of my car, I noticed him looking a little too hard, so I wanted to give him something to look at. I spread my legs open just enough for him to catch a glimpse of the pussy. I saw him instantly get hard, and a little smirk crossed my lips. I just had to edge him on, I couldn't help myself.

As I walked past him into the store, I reached my hand out and grabbed his stiffness and asked, "Can you fill her up, big boy?" He was as black as charcoal but somehow, I could still tell that my comment had him blushing. He acted like he was at a loss for words, so I let him go and went on into the store. After paying for my gas and picking up a couple of extra things, I went back out to my car and got in. I was looking around for the attendant, but he had disappeared, and it had me disappointed in a way. He was probably ducked off in some corner jacking his dick by now. I really wanted to get his number and maybe one day give him another tank to fill. I know I may have sounded like a straight whore, but I was just a horny bitch who liked to fuck. I liked to feel good and wouldn't allow anybody to stop that. I didn't give a fuck what other people thought.

When I finally made it to the office, I didn't see Jamal's car anywhere, and to be honest, I was actually relieved, although I did want to find out what was going on with him. It was odd for him to not be here because I had never known Jamal to miss a day of work. That alone had me feeling like something was off, but when I walked inside, I saw something even stranger. "Good morning, Miss Waters. Remember me?" I was staring into the face of Jamal's wife, who just happened to be sitting in my chair, waiting for me to come in. That bitch had her legs propped up on my desk with a devilish grin across her pouty lips.

I got to give it to Jamal. His wife was beautiful, so I could understand just why he never cheated on her. However, I didn't think there was a man or woman alive who could resist my sexual prowess. I almost felt like shit for fucking him, but that feeling went away quicker than it came. I then responded, "Yes. I remember you, Mrs. Jackson. Is there a reason you're sitting in my chair instead of your husband's?"

She let out a chuckle that kinda pissed me off, and then she stood up and walked over closer to where I was. "I can still smell my husband's dick on your breath." I wasn't sure what point this bitch was trying to make, but one of two things was about to happen. We were either going to fuck or fight, and I was down for either one.

"My husband had never cheated on me before you." She paused and continued, "So, I want to know what made you so special."

When she asked me that question, I had an immediate response. I got even closer and looked her straight in the eyes. "Why don't you let me show you, Mrs. Jackson?" I then sucked her bottom lip into my mouth and as I did this, I heard a noise behind me. I turned my head and noticed that Jamal had walked in.

I thought Terry would pull away from me, but instead, she continued to stand there, so I went back to molesting her pretty lips. I felt Jamal as he walked up behind me and reached around to caress my breasts. "Oh, y'all gonna start without me?"

When Jamal said those words, I knew right then that this had all been planned. Terry pulled back from me, but only to undo my skirt, making it fall to my feet. When Jamal pulled my shirt off, Terry went straight to my nipples. "Mmm, yes." As she sucked and pulled on my nipples really hard, Jamal, still behind me, reached down between my legs and began playing in my pussy. I could feel his hardness pressing against my ass cheeks. I never imagined the two of them doing something like this, but I was glad I was the one they were doing it to.

"You like that, Nicole?"

Jamal's voice made me tremble with excitement, and I knew my voice was shaky when I responded, "Yes. It feels so good. Please don't stop." Terry continued to suck my nipples like a pro, and then she reached her hand down to play in my pussy too. Jamal removed his hand but then pushed it back in between my legs from the back. I had to spread my legs a little just so he could get to my hole. I felt one of his long, fat fingers entering me, and at that same time, Terry dropped to her knees.

I gasped as she sucked my clit into her mouth. She let go of it, but only long enough to pull the hood back, and then she began flicking her tongue over the raw meat before sucking it back into her mouth. "Oh god, Mrs. Jackson, that shit feels so good."

My knees were getting weaker by the second, and I knew that I wouldn't be able to stand much longer. I tried to speak again, but I just couldn't get any more words out, so I leaned into Jamal instead as he said to his wife, "Suck that pussy good, baby."

I then turned my head to the side and reached my hand up behind his head so I could pull him down into a kiss, because kissing was my weakness. It always made me cum even harder, so I loved to do it.

I felt myself about to cum and wanted them to know it, so I pulled away from Jamal and said between breaths, "I'm cumming, please don't stop, I'm cumming." As Terry sucked on my clit harder, Jamal pushed his finger in and out of me faster. I came so hard that Jamal had to hold me up with his free arm to keep me from falling. When he pulled his finger out of me, he pushed it into my mouth, and I sucked all of my essence off of it. Jamal and Terry finally started getting undressed, and I knew then that things were about to get a lot freakier.

Terry sat her thick ass on my desk and lifted her legs up while spreading them apart. Her pussy was a soft pink color and perfectly formed. I wondered if it tasted as good as it looked, and my mouth watered at the thought. "Come suck this pussy like you sucked my husband's dick, Ms. Waters."

I looked at Jamal as if I was asking his permission, and he looked deep into my eyes and said, "Go ahead, Nicole. She's been waiting on this all weekend."

With that being said, I got between her legs and leaned over. I pushed the hood back from over her clit and sucked her swollen bud into my mouth. "Uh, mmm hmm." I heard Terry moan as I felt Jamal come up behind me and spread my ass cheeks open so he could prepare me for his big dick. He slapped me on my ass with the dick before sliding it into me, causing me to flinch. Terry and I moaned at the same time. "Mmm."

His dick felt bigger than it did the first time, or maybe I was just more into it this go round. As he went in and out of me, I could feel Terry's legs begin to tremble. I knew she was about to cum, so I prepared myself to taste her sweet nectar. Jamal started fucking me harder, causing his balls to swing and lightly tap my clit. He was slamming into me with deep aggression, and you could hear our bodies colliding with each thrust. They must have been in sync with each other, because they both began to cum at the same time.

Terry's cum tasted sweet on my tongue, and I wanted to make sure I got all of it. While drinking Terry's juice, I felt Jamal pull out and then shoot his cum all over my ass. He then used his dick to spread it out, as if he was putting mayonnaise on a sandwich. He stopped and then slapped me on my ass, as if he was punishing me for having good pussy. Terry then got up and got behind me to lick all of his cum off of me. That was a nasty bitch, and it turned me on even more.

I couldn't understand why Jamal had never set something up like this before. Maybe he didn't think that I would be down with it, or maybe he just never wanted to share his wife's good pussy. I was thankful, though, that he finally did. His wife was a freak, and I wanted to see him fuck her too and was ready to get down some more.

Sugar E. Wallz

Chapter Seven

"I know we ain't through already." I said the words out loud because I wanted to be heard.

Jamal and Terry looked at me, dumbfounded, and Jamal asked, "What the fuck you talking about, Nicole?"

I shook my head and let out a slight giggle. I walked over to Terry and pinched one of her nipples. I was so close up to her, it was as if we were in a face off. I put my fingers to my mouth and wet them, and then proceeded to play with Terry's nipple. I said, "Come on, Jamal, I want to see you fuck your wife's pretty ass pussy." This shit was bringing out the real freak in me. I continued, "I bet that big black dick of ours can fuck her pussy real good." Terry gave me a smile and then pulled me to her, kissing me.

Jamal came up behind his wife, and as we sandwiched her, I could hear her moaning, "Ah yeah. Mm hmm." Her moans made me even wetter, and when I moved my hand down between her thighs, she parted like the Red Sea.

Jamal backed away from us and said, "I'll be right back." Then he came back with a blanket that I never knew was in there. He laid it on the floor and then looked up at us. "Let's fuck," he said before getting on the blanket and lying down. His dick was standing at attention with pre-cum coming out of it. The light shined on it, giving it a glistening effect.

Terry and I looked at each other and said simultaneously, "Let's fuck." And then we walked over to where Jamal had the blanket to join him. Terry turned backwards with her ass facing Jamal, and then squatted down onto his massive member.

As he disappeared inside of her, I cupped his balls in my small hand and began massaging them. I looked Terry in the eyes and asked, "Does that dick feel good to you, Terry?"

She replied but never lost her rhythm. "Yes. Yes. This shit feels so good." As I played with his balls, I sucked one nipple at a time into my mouth, flicking my tongue over them and biting them. I then lay down on my stomach between Jamal's legs and sucked on Terry's clit. "Oh shit. Yes, you gonna make me cum." I wanted to make sure she understood why Jamal fucked me. My mouth and pussy game were on point. Plus, I wanted to make sure that this little rendezvous would happen again. I loved the sight of his dick going up inside of her, and although this wasn't the first time I watched some shit like this, it seemed to turn me on like it was. "Oh my god, I'm cumming, yes."

Hearing Terry say that made me suck on her clit even harder. My head bobbing up and down with her body didn't seem to faze me at all. I pulled back when she started trembling, and began playing with Jamal's balls again and watched as her white creamy cum coated the big black dick inside of her. "Oh. Oh yeah." Terry had slowed down and then finally stopped.

"Shit." That's all I heard Jamal say as he lay there, trying to catch his breath. I wondered if they really fucked each other like this at home, or did me being there watching them make it more interesting. Jamal had talked a lot about his wife but with a deep sense of respect. I never would have thought she would be this freaky. I also wondered if this was the first time that they shared each other with someone else. Something told me that I wasn't the first and damn sure wouldn't be the last.

Terry finally got up and then Jamal got up behind her. She came to me and said, "You know, Nicole, I knew you had fucked my husband that day I came here." She paused for a second and continued, "My husband never cheated on me. Everyone he fucks, we fuck together, so I was pissed." I started to respond to her, but she put a finger to my lips to hush me. "Y'all don't have to say anything. Just know from this day forward, if you want to fuck Jamal, you gotta fuck me too."

I was stunned but turned on at the same time. Terry removed her finger from over my lips, and I finally got the chance to speak. "Well, Mrs. Jackson, since you put it that way, let me know when you're ready for round two."

With that being said, I turned around and walked away to get dressed, leaving them to get dressed also. We had fucked the whole day away, but I wasn't complaining, because I was on the clock and would still be getting paid. I guess fucking the boss did have its good points. After Jamal and Terry got dressed and ready to leave, they said their goodbyes to me and Jamal told me to go home and get some rest, but I decided I would stay and try to get some work done, wet pussy and all.

Sugar E. Wallz

Chapter Eight

Because of the rendezvous with Jamal and his wife, I knew I would be behind on some reports that were due by the end of the week. I knew Jamal would have excused it, but I never had a deadline that I didn't meet, and there would be no exceptions. I loved my job but knew that one day I would want to explore other options. However, I hadn't ventured out anywhere else yet. I was determined to never be a statistic, and my mother kept me in school to ensure I would have a bright future. When I went to college, I knew a lot of the female students weren't very fond of me. They claimed I only made it through because I fucked a couple of the professors, but that shit was not true. Yeah, I fucked, but I did all of my own work and studied hard to get that degree. Fuck what they think, as long as I know. I couldn't help it that a couple of the professors were fine and well hung. I like to fuck and I like to cum, but making someone else cum was the ultimate pleasure. At least I wasn't walking around with a bunch of babies by different men. Nor was I making visits to the health department to treat a damn venereal disease. Hell no. I was disease and baby free, and I had a good career. Until all of that changed, I was going to live my life to the fullest extent.

It was beginning to get late and I was getting tired, but I wanted to finish this one last report. I was working on getting Jamal another big investor, so my work had to be on point. I had made Jamal a lot of money over the years, sometimes by my presence alone, and when Jamal got paid good, I got paid good too. My exotic features and fat ass made his clients do double takes and got them to sign contracts, mainly just to be in my vicinity again. I was blessed with beauty and sex appeal and used it to my advantage.

After finishing the last report, I decided I should call it a night because another day would be awaiting me in a few short hours. However, before I gathered my things, I decided to get one last bit of pleasure before leaving. I pushed my chair a little ways from the desk and propped one leg up on the arm rest and leaned back. I wanted to take my time with this one, so I pulled the hood back on my clit and started massaging it in slow circular motions. "Sss, yes."

That shit was feeling so good, and I knew it wouldn't take me long to cum at this rate.

I started going a little faster and felt myself getting a dizzy feeling, when all of a sudden, I heard a noise. I stopped and opened my eyes, and then suddenly, out of nowhere, someone appeared. "Damn," I said, startled. I had forgotten that Jamal had hired a nighttime security officer a few months prior. He walked right in on me and it caused me to blush with embarrassment, something I never did. The office was slightly dim, but his chocolate skin seemed to radiate a soft glow as he stood there watching me. I just smiled, because I simply couldn't think of anything else to do.

He didn't say a word to me, but instead, just stood there looking at my exposed pussy, so I said, "Fuck it," and began massaging my swollen clit again. If he arrested me for indecent exposure, it would have damn well been worth it. I had a smirk on my face and asked him, "Is there something wrong, Officer?" I paused and looked at him lustfully before finishing, "You act like you've never seen a girl play with her pussy before."

He looked from my eyes to my pussy before responding, "Ms. Waters, this is not the time nor place for that, so you're in violation."

He came closer and when he got right up on me, I pushed my finger into my pussy hole and stated, "Well, arrest me then." I was so far into my zone until I didn't even remember his name. When he pulled out his cuffs, I stopped what I was doing and stood up. I licked the pussy juice off of my finger before turning around and putting my hands behind my back so that I could be restrained. Just the mere thought of it had me even more excited.

Before placing the cuffs around my wrists, he said, in a demanding tone, "I'm going to need to search you first, so I need you to put your hands against the wall and spread your legs apart." He didn't have to tell me twice, because I submitted to his demands instantly. My nipples stood at attention as soon as he ran his hands around my breasts. He squeezed them lightly and then told me, "It feels as if you have something hidden in your shirt, so I'm gonna need you to remove it." I happily obliged and removed the sheer top that I had on. When I did this, he pulled on my nipples with his fingers and said, "These are very sharp, Ms. Waters, and could really hurt someone." He then told me to remove the rest of my clothes, which actually wasn't anything more than the wrap-around skirt. I untied it and let it fall to the floor and then put my hands back on the wall, assuming the proper position.

As his smooth hands found their way over my naked body, my pussy became instantly wet. "Okay, you can put your hands behind your back now," he said in a demanding voice. I did as I was told with no questions asked and was placed in hand restraints. After cuffing me, he said, "I know you're hiding something, so it seems that I'll have to do a cavity search to find it."

I looked at him and smiled and said, "Well, I guess you gotta do your job then. I hope you find what you're looking for." He walked me over to my desk and forcefully bent me over it and spread my ass cheeks. He pushed his long, slender finger into my pussy and began moving it around, and then he pushed his thumb into my asshole, giving me an instant rush. "Shit." I hesitated for only a second, and then said, "You may need an instrument a little bigger than that to find what you're looking for."

He continued to move his fingers in and out of me for a couple of minutes. His fingers were long and slender and made my insides creamy. He finally pulled out his fingers and stated in an authoritative tone, "You're right, Ms. Waters. It seems that I'll have to use something else so I can search a little deeper."

With that said, he pushed the thickest dick I had ever felt inside of me. "Uh." It felt like he had ripped me open, and that shit actually hurt a little bit, but once he started going good, the pain turned to instant pleasure. He was sliding his dick in and out of me with great precision. His long, deep strokes had me feeling high, like I had been on a three-day binge. I wanted so bad to reach down and play with my clit while he was fucking me, but the handcuffs were keeping me restrained, so I couldn't do anything but take the dick he was giving.

"You like this big dick, Ms. Waters?"

He was tearing my pussy up, and I told him between thrusts, "Yes...uh, uh, yes. I...I...love this...this dick. Yes." However, I wanted him to take the damn cuffs off so that I could explore. I felt him begin to slow his rhythm and then grab a hold of them. I then felt him unlocking them while his dick was still stuffed inside of me.

Once the cuffs were off, he pulled out of my pussy, but his dick was still standing at full attention. I turned around to face him and then wrapped my hand around his girth. His dick was beautiful, and I knew I had to get a taste of it. I went down on my knees and began licking the head while cupping his balls in my hand and slowly massaging them. There was no way I would be able to put his whole dick in my mouth, it was just too much. So, I took in what I could. "Suck that dick, baby. Mmm hmm." He grabbed the back of my head, pulling me into him while he fucked my mouth. His enormous dick almost caused me to gag. When his vein started pulsing, I knew he was close to cumming, and I couldn't wait to swallow his seeds. "Catch this cum, girl. Shit." He showed me no mercy as his cum shot down my throat, and like the bad bitch that I was, I swallowed all of it.

After sucking each and every drop out of him, I got up off my knees and asked, "So, Officer, does this mean I got time served?"

A small chuckle came from deep within him, and then he replied, "I'm going to request that you get probation, and if you violate, the punishment will be very severe." With that said, he turned around and walked out.

It had been a long day and I was completely exhausted, so I got dressed, gathered my things, and went home to get me some much-needed rest. I was sure there would be much more exciting things for me to get into the next day, and I couldn't wait to see what tomorrow brought.

Chapter Nine

When I made it home and walked in my front door, I immediately started stripping. I wanted to take a hot bath instead of a shower, because I just wanted to lie back and relax all of my muscles and meditate. I didn't know what direction my life was taking, but I knew I needed a change, and a long, hot bath would clear my head so I could try to get my priorities straight.

As the tub was filling up, I went into the living room to check my messages, but there was nothing worth listening to on the machine. I thought Jamal would have at least checked on me by now, but there was no word from him.

I walked back into the bathroom and submerged myself into the hot water. My muscles were still a little stiff from so much action, and the water soothed them perfectly. I leaned my head on the back of the tub and began to reminisce on all of the lovers I'd had and the different things that each of them brought to my life. I had an amazing experience with each of them. I wondered if I would ever just want one lover, but the thought quickly left my mind. For now, I was satisfied with things just the way they were. As I was soaking in the water, my eyes began to slowly close. As I drifted off to sleep, my body began to twitch and dreams began to take over my mind.

The party was jumping and the music was flowing. Men and women of all colors, shapes, and sizes were dancing and having the time of their lives. As I walked in, all eyes were on me, as if I was some sort of alien, and in all actuality, I was. I was intruding on their territory, not the other way around, so they had every right. I didn't know anyone and they didn't know me, but we all shared the same thoughts. Everyone in the room was naked, and yet, I was still standing there clothed. For once in my life, I was afraid to get undressed. I ventured further inside and noticed a few people going into a room off to the side. I couldn't help myself because I had always been nosy. I needed to see what was behind that door, so I followed. I was so shocked at what I saw, and I just stood there. It was a complete orgy with men fucking men, women fucking women, and male and female couples. I had never seen this many people in their own world fucking all at once.

I suddenly felt my clothes being stripped away, and there was nothing I could do to stop it from happening. Then, I felt something wet on my nipple. There was a dark-skinned dread with my left nipple in his mouth and a light-skinned guy with my right one in his. Both of them sucking on my nipples at the same time had me in another world. My clit swelled at the sensation and poked out from between my pussy lips. I was beginning to break into a sweat when I suddenly felt someone spread my pussy and suck my clit in between their lips. I was too overwhelmed with passion to even look down and see who was violating me in such a way. I only knew that I was feeling good at that very moment. "Yes. Oh my god. Yes," I said so low that I didn't think they heard me.

I felt myself being picked up and carried, and then finally placed in the middle of a big bed. I happened to see who the third culprit was and saw that it was a female. Once they placed me on the bed, they began to violate me once again. None of them said a word to me, they just continued on with their exploration. The female spread my legs open and inserted two fingers into my pussy, as the two men twisted my nipples and watched. I was overcome with desire as she sucked my swollen bud back into her mouth. The light-skinned dude positioned himself behind her and rammed his dick into her, causing her to cringe. I watched as he fucked her, and he turned me on so much that it caused me to summon over the sexy dread. He got on his knees over me and straddled my face, and as his balls hung over my mouth, I sucked one in. As I let it go and sucked the other one into my mouth, I reached up and began to jack his dick. His balls were a perfect fit, and I sucked them like the professional I was.

I heard the light-skinned dude talking shit to the female between my legs while their skin was slapping together. "Take this dick. Make this dick cum, bitch."

I felt myself about to cum, so I sucked on his balls a little harder and jacked his dick a little faster. I wanted him to cum too. Dread didn't disappoint me either. As his warm cum shot out all over my face, my cum squirted out all over hers. I took my hands and rubbed it in like it was skin cream. I licked the remainder off of his dick and cleaned him up. As the dread moved from over me, the light-skinned guy pulled out and cum shot all over her back and my stomach. I loved watching a nigga shoot him cum. That shit turned me on. I wanted to have these two fine men to myself, so I pushed her up off of me. She could tell by the look in my eyes that her time was up. She didn't say anything when she walked away. She only smiled and waved. I knew she wanted to stay but tonight, she would have to join in on someone else's dream, because I was tired of mine being invaded.

I said to the dread, "I want you to lie down." I straddled him on my feet as the light-skinned guy got behind me and reached around to play with my clit. I was so wet that when I squatted down, the dread's dick slid right inside of me. I began to slide up and down on his dick slowly, because I wanted to enjoy the moment.

"Ride that dick, just like that," the dread said while looking me in the eyes. I felt the light-skinned guy come behind me and do something I didn't expect. He spread my ass cheeks and slowly slid his dick in my ass. I had been in a lot of sexual predicaments, but never on like this. I had seen it done before and had always wondered how a bitch could take two dicks. Even in my dreams, I had to admit that this shit felt too good. I rode the hell out of those dicks, and the pressure from it made me feel light headed. I knew that when I finally came, it was going to be explosive and boy, was I right. "Oh shit, y'all. I'm about to cum." The one behind me had to hold me up when I came because of the intensity. They then pushed me off of them and came all over my back and stomach at the same time.

At that same moment, I jerked awake and reached down between my legs. The dream felt so real, and I could see my cum swirling around in the water. It seemed as if I had been in the tub for hours, and I didn't want to get out, but I knew I had to. I hoped that when I fell asleep again I would have a dream that surpassed the one I just had. When I got out of the tub, I felt real sluggish and didn't even bother drying off. However, when I made it to my bed, I couldn't even fall asleep because I kept thinking about my dream.

I decided I would read my newspaper because I hadn't had a chance to read it yet. So much bad news covered the front page and I couldn't handle it right now, so I flipped to the entertainment section. I noticed an advertisement for a concert being held by an up-and-coming underground artist, and since it had been a while since I had been to one, I figured I would go. I needed a change of scenery, but I knew I would need to go shopping first. Whenever I went, I had to make sure I outdid everyone in the room. I knew there would be niggas from all over, so I had to make sure I looked my best.

I didn't want to go by myself, though, so I decided I would go see Remy the next day and ask her to go with me. It would also be a nice little change for her. Who knows, I might even be able to get a taste of that sweet little pussy again, and we could bring us back a nice little treat. With thoughts of the concert and a night with Remy in my head, I drifted off to sleep.

Chapter Ten

When the alarm clock went off, I woke up, feeling as if I hadn't even been to sleep. I knew I needed to get up, although I wanted to stay in bed all day long. I lay there for a few minutes and decided that I was going to call the office and tell them that I wasn't coming in today. I figured as good as I fucked them, I should be able to get anything I wanted with no questions asked.

I rolled over and picked up my phone and dialed the number to the office, only to be greeted by the answering service, so I left a message letting them know that my ass was incognito. I knew that Jamal wouldn't be mad because I had never called in before. Hell, I don't even remember ever taking a sick day. I stopped thinking about the office and started thinking about this pussy. It was time for my morning nut, so I reached down between my legs and began to play with my clit. "Mmm," I moaned and pressed on it really hard, causing my heart to speed up with excitement. I stuck my finger into my hole to wet it and then put it back on my swollen clit. I wanted to cum hard this morning, so I masturbated it faster than usual.

I imagined that one day I would get tired of waking up like this and would have someone beside me handling all of this, but for now, I was content doing my own thing. I decided not to use big boy that I kept in the drawer, but instead, I would use my little bullet. It was small, but it could handle some of the biggest jobs. I turned it on and placed it against my clit. The vibration alone turned me on even more. I pulled the hood back and then stretched my legs out completely straight. I tightened my ass cheeks so that it would be more intense, and came quicker than anticipated. When I came, I lay completely still with only my right hand moving. My heart was steady beating faster while small beads of sweat began to form on my forehead. I came so hard I thought I would go into cardiac arrest. It took me a few minutes to gain my breath back to a steady pace, and as I lay there like I was paralyzed, I drifted back to sleep.

When I woke up again, the time had flown by and half of the day was gone. However, it wasn't too late for shopping, and I knew a few stores that would be open, so I got up, took my shower, and got myself together before leaving out. I decided to get up with Remy afterwards because I didn't have time to go see her now. We would have to pick her up something the next day.

I pulled up to my favorite shop, called Martinas, where only the best name brands were sold. When I walked in, my favorite host greeted me. She knew that when I came in I was going to spend a lot of money, making her commission check real nice. She also loved the taste of my pussy, and I made sure to serve her with it every time. I found a sleek, money-green Versace bodysuit that formed to each and every curve. I knew that wearing it would make me stand out above all the other females. I went into the dressing room and the host followed. I tried on the body suit and when I put it on, all she said was, "Nice."

I thanked her and took it off, and then sat down in front of the full-length mirror while she sat on the bench in front of me. I lifted my leg up and watched the reflection of my pussy open, and said, "I got something right here a little nicer." She dropped to her knees and began flicking her tongue over my clit as I watched her through the mirror. "Yes, suck this pussy. Oh, it feels so good." I didn't care that I was in a dressing room in the middle of a store. I needed to let this bitch know how I felt. I felt myself about to cum and put my hand on the back of her head so she couldn't pull back. "I'm about to cum. Keep sucking. Oh, yes." I came all in her mouth as my body trembled, and she cleaned up every drop when we finished. I got dressed and walked out of the dressing room, smiling as usual. I could tell that the other customers knew what happened by the looks on their faces, but I didn't give a fuck what they thought.

I paid for my purchases and walked out, bumping into a blast from my past. The sexy dark dread from the strip club was right there before me and for some reason, his presence took my breath away. "What's up, lil' mama? Don't I know you from somewhere?"

His voice did something to me and made me feel things inside that I had never felt before. I became wet instantly, but the wetness felt different than any before. My insides started tingling, and I didn't know what the fuck was happening, but I knew that I had to get away from him. "Um, I don't think so. I have somewhere I gotta be. Sorry." And with that said, I hurried to my car and drove away. I could still feel the effects of him when I pulled up to the club Remy danced at. I had to get a hold of myself and try to get him out of my head, and there was no better way to do that than watching a bitch shake their ass. This was also my opportunity to see if Remy wanted to go to the concert. As always, I walked up and bypassed everyone in line. The scene looked a little different from the week before, but the vibe still felt the same. I went to the bar to get a drink and asked the bartender if Remy had gone on stage yet.

He replied, "Nah, that fine wine is in the private room up in VIP." He then told me where to go, and I headed in that direction.

Going up the spiral staircase was an adventure all on its own. Transparent boxes surrounded it and each one contained a naked dancer. Some actually danced to the music while some masturbated themselves for all to see. I looked down and saw the dancer that was on the stage and when I looked, it was almost as if she could feel me, because she looked up at me at the same time. I smiled, shook my head, and kept going to my destination. I found the VIP room the bartender told me Remy was in and didn't even bother to knock. I just walked in like I owned the place.

I recognized the fat ass as soon as I saw it. Remy was bent over, sucking on some dude's dick while he had his hand on the back of her head, pushing her into him. She must have felt my presence, because she looked directly at me and once we locked eyes, nothing needed to be said.

I walked up behind her and ran a finger up and down the length of her ass crack and then down to her pussy lips. She moaned in pleasure, "Mmm hmm." The nigga she was sucking on didn't say anything. He winked at me and smiled when I began taking my clothes off. After getting undressed, I hopped onto the couch where he was sitting, grabbed the back of his head, and pulled him into my pussy. He didn't even protest as he licked and sucked my pussy real slow. I was thrusting my hips into his face when Remy finally came up from the dick. My eyes grew large because the size of his dick was insane, and I knew that Remy's mouth had to be tired. After she lifted herself off his face and stood over him in front of Remy, I bent over and kissed her on the lips, and asked, "You ready for this?"

She smiled at me and nodded her head. I spread my pussy lips and squatted down. As my pussy opened up, his dick began to disappear inside of it. As soon as his dick was in me, another man appeared and walked over to us. This was a white man, and although I wasn't into white meat, this cracker had some swagger. He was sexy and looked gangsta as fuck with all of his tattoos. He was giving me a whole new outlook on white men. As soon as he got over to us, he began undoing his pants and pulled his dick out, saying, "Y'all mind if I join?"

I had always heard that white men had small dicks, but after seeing what he was working with, I had a whole different outlook. It had to be a myth, because this cracker was hung.

I wanted to see him fuck Remy, so I told her, "Bend over baby, put a little creamer in this coffee." She bent over with her ass in the air and then brought her mouth to my pussy. As she sucked on my clit while I rode the mandingo, the white boy positioned himself behind her. He grabbed a hold of her hips and rammed his dick inside of her. I could feel her jerk from the width of him. He began pushing into her full force, and her face was steady pounding into me, causing friction with the man under me. I could hear their bodies connecting, and the sound of it gave me a whole new rhythm. He reached his arms out and started pulling and twisting on my hardened nipples as I rode the other dick to ecstasy. The pressure of the dick and Remy's tongue had me ready to cum.

I looked at the white boy and told him, "Fuck her pussy harder and then cum with me." He did just as I asked and began fucking her with a vengeance. He was fucking her so hard that she had to grab a hold of my legs to keep her balance, and she had to also release my clit from her mouth. However, it didn't stop my flow. I took one last look at the white boy, leaned my head back, and came all over the dick inside of me, "Oh, shit. Yes."

At that same moment, the white boy pulled out of Remy and shot his cum all over her ass and back. He came so hard that some of it shot all the way on me, and the nigga under me took his hands and rubbed it all over my nipples. This was the type of shit I lived for, and I was so glad I decided to come here. This little escapade also made me forget about the dark-skinned dread that continued to try and invade my thoughts. I couldn't figure out what it was he was doing to me, but I knew that it would take much more than this to forget about him, and I was determined to find something that would work.

When we were done and the guys left, I talked to Remy about going to the concert, and she was excited that I asked her to go. She then told me about a party the white boy had told her about when she first came across him in the club. He told her it was a BDSM party, and since neither of us had ever been introduced to it, we decided that we would check it out. I had heard about BDSM and knew that it was all types of sexual pleasures going on at the same time. Me being the curious woman that I was needed to see it for myself. I was always game to try new things but had always thought that only white people indulged in that kind of stuff. The white boy had told Remy that all ages and races would be there participating, and it was safe, good, clean fun. We decided that we would only try what interested us, and if we didn't like the scene, we would leave. The party was two days away, and it would be more than we bargained for.

Sugar E. Wallz

Chapter Eleven

It was hard to find a place to park because the whole yard was already packed. Even the street in front of the house was lined up with vehicles. The people I saw getting out of these cars were dressed very differently than what we expected and made us feel like we were overdressed. However, we were still going to join in on this event and explore the extraordinary. I finally found a parking spot after driving around for several minutes, but it was way over in the next block. Maybe walking would do us a bit of good and get our adrenaline flowing.

We walked past a dude sitting on the hood of a car, getting his dick sucked out in the open, and didn't seem to have a care in the world. He acted as if no one else was around, and the girl that was bent over sucking his dick didn't even slow down or let up at all. The white bitch was the definition of deep throat, because she was swallowing the whole thing and his dick was far from small. We continued walking until we got to the door of the house where the party was being held ,and when we got there, knots began to form in our stomachs. When we got to the door, we knocked but the music coming from inside was so loud, I'm sure no one heard us. About that time, two dudes holding hands walked around us and walked right in, leaving the door open behind them, which to me was an invitation to walk right in behind them. Once inside, we were shocked at what we found.

There were people everywhere, all having sex in the open. No one came to greet us as we stood there, so we decided to explore and find out what else was going on in here. As we walked around, we noticed people going into different rooms, each with a different color door. We tried to stop some people walking past to try and find out what was going on behind the doors, but no one acknowledged us, leaving us to find out what was going on ourselves.

There were six doors and we decided that we would find out what was behind each one of them. There was a mini bar in the middle of the room, so before we started exploring, we went over to get a drink. The bartender was topless and had a gold ring in each of her nipples. She was attractive and mysterious at the same time, making the combination scary. We each got a shot of gin that was so strong it felt like our throats were on fire. The bartender then offered each of us a little pill and stated, "It makes the first time a little easier."

I refused the pill but Remy popped one and then took the one offered to me into her pocket. I looked at her crazy as she said, "Just in case." I shrugged my shoulders and we walked away from the bar to begin our journey

We went to the yellow door first and prepared ourselves for whatever was behind it. I walked in first with Remy close behind me, and we saw a table with all kinds of sex toys laid out on it. Surrounding the table were ten beds, but only four of them had people in them. The people in the beds continued their escapades as if we were not there, so we ventured closer to get a better look.

One of the beds had two women in it with one of them wearing a strap-on that had two dicks instead of one. She was fucking the girl in front of her in both holes, and I had to admit that the bitch was putting it down. Remy and I made eye contact with her as she pounded on the other female. It was as if us looking at her made her angry, because she began to fuck the woman even harder. She fucked her like a man, and that shit was making my pussy wet. Remy moved a little closer to me as if she were scared of something. I grabbed her hand and pulled her away so we could check out the action on the next bed.

On this bed, we found a man chained to the bedpost with his ass pointing up in the air. His dick and balls were being devoured by a man that lay beneath him. There was also a woman behind him pushing a string of beads into his asshole and then pulling them back out. The man under him was jacking his own dick while he sucked the other man's into his mouth. I had seen a lot of shit in my lifetime, but I never saw a man suck another man's dick. Something just never seemed right about it, but they say a man does it better than a woman, because since they have a dick of their own, they know what another man likes. I watched, thinking that maybe I could learn a new technique.

He pulled the head into his mouth and sucked it so hard his cheeks sunk in. He didn't use his free hand to hold it but instead, used it to pull and squeeze on the guy's balls really hard. So hard I thought he would rip them off. The dick disappeared so far down his throat, and as the woman behind him yanked the string of beads from his ass, he started jerking and I knew then that he was cumming. The guy that was sucking him must have swallowed every single drop, because I never saw any of the cum leave his mouth. I was really trying to keep my composure, at least until I explored every room, but I ain't gonna lie, my pussy was soaking wet. I didn't know how much longer I could contain my sexual lusts.

Remy and I continued on to the next bed where there was an older man and woman. The old man held a burning candle in his wrinkled hand and was tilting it so that the hot wax could drip down on his companion's hardened nipples. The old lady was massaging the man's shriveled up dick and trying really hard to make it wake up. I felt really bad for her because she looked like she wanted it really bad. I remembered the pill the bartender gave Remy and told her to give it to the old man, hoping it would help the situation. Remy gave him the pill as the lady kept pulling on his dick with her small, wrinkled hands.

I told the old lady that maybe she should try sucking on it, so she did. The combination of the pill and her warm mouth seemed to be making it grow a little harder. It wasn't that big and caused me to wonder how something so small could please her, but then I got to thinking that maybe she just never had bigger. After he became fully erect, the old lady turned around and got on all fours. He got behind her and went straight in, and we watched for only a second as the muscles in his little wrinkled ass began flexing. Before we walked away, she turned her head to us and mouthed, "Thank you." I prayed at that same moment for a man who could keep it going even after we were walking around on canes. The old man seemed to be okay now, so we left them there to handle their business and moved on to the next scene.

The last bed we came to had three females on it, and my pussy became drenched as soon as I saw them. One of them was lying on their back while another was riding her face and the other one was eating her. Remy and I watched as the woman between her legs sucked her clit into her mouth. It looked as if she were french kissing the little bud. She moved her head from side to side, pulling on it with her lips, then she would release it and lick the whole pussy. She licked all the way to her asshole and back. She then inserted her fingers, sliding them in and out as the pussy juice coated them. That bitch was eating the hell out of that pussy, and I was getting more turned on by the second.

The woman that was riding her face grabbed Remy's hand to pull her up on the bed. Remy looked at me as if asking for permission, so I said, "Go ahead. I'll be there in a minute." She hurried and got undressed and then climbed onto the bed. The woman pulled a dildo out from somewhere and began rubbing it against Remy's pussy. I watched as Remy's clit grew with excitement and began to poke out from between her pussy lips. I got on the bed behind the woman eating the pussy, and first started by licking her ass crack and then went down to the pussy. She tasted sweet against my tongue, and then I stuck a finger into her ass, pulling and pushing slowly as she pushed her ass back against the pressure. I looked up at Remy and watched as she rotated her hips to the dildo that was inside of her. I already knew that she could ride one with expertise, but to watch her do it while someone else pushed it into her drove me crazy. The one who was lying down getting her face rode grabbed onto Remy's legs as she fucked the other woman's pussy with her tongue. Only a couple of minutes passed and amazingly, all five of us came at the same time. I came so hard that it literally took my breath away. Remy collapsed on her knees, and the one who was in front of me just put her head down in exhaustion. The one who was riding the woman's face fell back, trying to gain a breath. Wet pussy aroma filled the air around us. Remy and I took a second before we got up and got dressed. There was still so much more to see, and I couldn't wait to keep going. The next door was the color green, and we were anxious to see what we would find.

When we walked into the green room, the layout was intriguing. There was a lone bed in the middle of the floor and one female sat upon it. Surrounding her were four different men, and all of them had their dicks out in their hands. The female was on her back and spread her pussy open once she saw us walking up to her. She stuck two fingers into her mouth and licked them before pushing them into her pussy, pushing them in and then pulling them out while looking me in the eyes. Her eyes were the color of the sky on a clear day and had me hypnotized. She took the fingers of her other hand and pulled on her clit really hard. She pulled on it so hard I thought she was going to detach it from her pussy. The men around her began jacking their dicks, and then she got up on all fours and went from one dick to the other. Slurping and sucking on each one for a minute before going to the next one. As she sucked the last one, another one entered her from behind. Sticking his dick in so deep you would have thought her heart would burst. The other two men continued jacking off, and then they all switched places, all of them alternating from her mouth to her pussy. They fucked her long and hard, and it was definitely a sight to see.

The men started jerking in unison, and then all of them came on her body at the same time. She then rubbed their cum all over her body, like a body wash. The shit was actually kinda sexy, but it wasn't something me and Remy wanted any part of, so we left and went on to the next room, which would be behind a blue door. Inside this room, there was a woman who stood to be about six feet tall with a whip and a black leather, crotchless bodysuit, and her breasts swung freely. I was freaky but could never understand how someone could get turned on by being beaten with a whip, but to each their own. It was just something I never desired. The man in front of her was on the floor on all fours with a dog leash around his neck. When she hit him with the whip, I jumped as if it was me she hit instead. She demanded, "Get up on your knees and suck my pussy like a good boy."

He got right up on his knees and sucked each pussy lip before flicking his tongue over her clit like an ice cream cone. She grabbed the back of his head and said, "You better suck this pussy right and make me cum. And you better not waste any of it, or you will pay." He began sucking harder until her legs began to tremble and when she was done, he got back on all fours. She then pulled out a small vibrator and ordered him to open his ass cheeks. When he did, she pushed the vibrator in and out with great force. Remy and I were shocked. We looked at each other and without saying a word, we knew what the other was saying. It was time to get out of there, so we moved on to the next room.

Chapter Twelve

This room was much smaller than the other ones we had been in, and we were completely blown away at what we found when we entered. The room was full of people who had breasts, dicks, and pussies. I knew what a hermaphrodite was but had never seen one up close, but now I had me a front row seat. It was really strange seeing the dick and pussy combination, but we couldn't turn away from them. We stared in shock as they fucked each other. One of them had their dick in the other's pussy and was jacking that person's dick at the same time. They didn't have balls or even clits, so it was really funny to look at. They were all in different positions, and we wanted to get a better look, so we got closer.

As we walked up, one of them put their parts on full display for us. We giggled at the sight, imagining having the best of both worlds. We looked on as one was sucking another's dick while he rolled his nipples between his fingers. His breasts were huge, but his dick was really small. We had enough and didn't want to stay in this room any longer. The scene just wasn't our flavor, so we journeyed on to the next adventure.

We left there and went to the room with the purple door. There was a chair in the middle of the room that was shaped like the throne of a king. A fine ass nigga with a big dick and a crown on his head sat in that chair. There was loud music playing, and six naked women surrounded the chair, dancing on stripper poles. His dick was rock hard and standing at attention, so Remy and I walked over to get a closer look and to hopefully cop a feel. When we got up on him, he looked at us crazy and then said, "We don't wear clothes in this room. Get undressed."

We did exactly as we were told. My pussy was already wet and throbbing from watching all the sex scenes we had already seen in the other rooms. He ordered, "Spread your legs and open your pussy lips for me."

He was so intoxicating, and all I could do was follow his orders. I was finding it very hard to turn him down. My pussy was soaking wet, but I still flinched as he took two of his fingers and entered me. His fingers were long and soft and felt so good inside of my walls. He looked at Remy and said, "Get behind her."

She bent down behind me and spread my ass cheeks and began licking my asshole. As she did this, one of the dancers quit dancing and got behind Remy and placed a strap-on around Remy's wide hips. I already knew what was about to happen and braced myself. I bent over and wrapped my hand around his dick and then licked the pre-cum off of the tip. I then ran my tongue up and down his shaft and traced the head of his dick. I felt Remy enter me from behind. She grabbed my hips and went in and out of me slowly. The strap-on she wore was purple, like almost everything else in the room, and it left no part of my insides untouched. Every time she slid inside of me, I would let his dick slide down my throat. Remy and I were in sync, as always.

I wanted to feel a real dick inside of me now, so I pushed Remy out of me and stood up. I turned around and faced her and then sucked one nipple at a time between my lips. The nigga in the chair pulled me to him and began fingering my asshole as he slowly guided his dick inside of my pussy. The pleasure of his thickness felt so good and caused me to reach down and touch myself. He pulled out of my pussy and went in my ass, and since Remy still had on the strap-on, I said to her, "Come fuck this pussy, Remy." And, of course, she never disappointed. The slow rhythm of the dick and strap-on together caused me to cum quickly. "Oh shit, I'm cum-ming. Yes."

As I began cumming all over the strap-on, they began fucking me harder, not letting up until I was weak and empty. When I was done, I wanted Remy to enjoy what I just had. After the man cleaned up, he pulled Remy to him, and I placed the strap-on around me. We give Remy the same pleasure I just experienced. She pinched her nipples as they bounced around on her chest. We fucked Remy until she came and when we were done, Remy and I got dressed and left to explore the last room.

This room was orange and gave us chills as soon as we entered. There was a St. Andrews cross nailed to the wall, and a woman was on it chained up by her wrists and ankles. Her legs were slightly spread apart. She had clamps on her nipples and a clamp attached to her clit, all of them connected and joined by a long linked chain. There was a man sitting in front of her that kept pulling the chain about every thirty seconds, and every time he pulled, she cried out. When he noticed us, he pulled on them even harder. "Agh. Agh." The woman's cries became louder, and then he lightened up.

He did this several times and then the woman began cumming, all of her juices sliding down between her thighs, coating her skin. We had finally had enough of this house for one day. We knew we would never journey back here again. This was definitely not the type of place we wanted to be. I decided that I would take Remy to a real party, without all that extra bullshit. One that she would truly enjoy. So, instead of taking her home, I took her to one of my long-time acquaintance's house and had every intention of giving her the time of her life.

Sugar E. Wallz

Chapter Thirteen

I pulled up to my acquaintance's house and got out of the car, telling Remy to follow me. She asked, "What are we going to do here?"

I told her, "Have a good time. Let's go." We walked to the door hand in hand, and we heard a lot of laughter. I gathered my thoughts and walked in as if I owned this place. The living room was huge and everyone looked up as we invaded their space. I introduced Remy to everyone and told Travis, "I want her to have the time of her life today. Can you help me out?"

He smiled and said, "You know you came to the right place." He then told the girl next to him to go in the back room and grab some blankets out of the closet. She did as he asked and when she re-entered the living room, I could see a small yet nervous smile cross Remy's lips, highlighting her beautiful face. Travis told everyone in the room, "Let's get undressed and have some fun."

His boy Mark wasted no time and was the first to take his clothes off. His lean body was cut with muscle, and his cropped hair was neat, as always. His dick was already semi-hard with anticipation. His girl quickly followed suit and undressed very fast. Her small breasts were slightly pointed up with her nipples hard enough to cut through glass. Her pussy was already glistening with wetness. Next came John, who was acting a little more reserved. He finally got there and pushed his pants and boxers down quickly to his feet. As he stepped out of them, he looked around and glanced at all of us watching. He stared at us as he slid his feet back in his shoes. His dick was staring at us, too, as it stuck out, erect, ready for action. I could hear Remy gasp behind me, "Holy shit." The length of him startling her.

Remy's eyes were wide and her mouth slightly open as she began to breathe a little heavier. I turned and grabbed her hand, walking her all the way into the room now. Her big, beautiful eyes took in the scene, and I swear I could see her cheeks turning pink as sweat appeared lightly on her forehead.

The girl who brought the blankets in began spreading them out on the floor and then dropped to get them right. She then got up and gathered all her things, said something to Travis, and then walked out. The rest of us mere inches away, our eyes questioning what just happened, but our lips not wanting to speak it out loud. Three very hard dicks and three wet pussies were ready for a night of fun. We all continued on as if she was never there.

I could feel Remy's breath on my neck and turned to her. I could still see the slight smile on her face and the excitement in her eyes. Her nipples were hard under her shirt, making me want to rip it off and pull one into my mouth. I finally undressed and, of course, she followed. I noticed that the room was eerily quiet but tried not to let it mess up my groove. Sue's nipples were hard enough to cut glass, but Remy's could definitely cut through steel. Mark walked over and reached from behind me, brushing his fingers over my nipples. John told me to bring Remy to him, and I did as he said. She stood in front of him with her legs slightly parted.

I knew her pussy was wet and could see her little clit seeking out beyond her pussy lips. I told her to lie down, and she happily obliged. She looked up and saw the dicks hovering above her and then turned to look at me. I could tell that she was still a little nervous, and I winked at her. I wanted to put her at ease so she could really enjoy herself. I placed a hand on each knee and spread her legs. Her beautiful pussy opened up just for me.

Her pussy lips were swollen and I could see her wetness coating all the way down to her asshole. John and Mark kneeled down beside her head, with one on each side, dicks held out over her face. Remy grabbed each one, and they were now so close they're almost touching. I saw her eyes close and her tongue dart out of her mouth, resting in between the two dick heads. "Mmm hmm," I heard her moan as she opened her eyes and looked at me once again.

I smiled and said, "You ready baby?" as I bent over between her legs and buried my face into her pussy. It tasted sweet, as usual, and I covered her clit with my whole tongue as her hips rose up to meet my mouth. I cut my eyes up toward her as she was sucking on both of the dick heads. I slid two fingers into her wet hole and moved them slowly in and out while applying pressure to her swollen clit.

Sue was standing there with her hands on her hips and her nipples still rock hard. She had on a strap-on and with the taste of Remy's pussy on my lips, I watched as she twisted and pulled on her nipples. I could hear Remy slurping on the dicks, and my pussy kept getting wetter. I looked up into Remy's eyes again, and her beautiful brown eyes seemed to be begging me to rescue her. I came up and called her name and then reached my hand out for her to take. She let the dicks fall out of her hands and gripped mine as the men stared at me crazy. When I pulled her up, she wrapped her arms around my neck and held tight, as if I was a superhero who just saved her from a villain. Then, suddenly, she kissed my lips. She reached down and rubbed on my clit, but I slapped her on the ass and moved her hand away, because we would have our time soon enough.

Sue came over and lay down on the blanket, the strap-on still dangling from her hips. When she laid down, I stood Remy over her where she was straddling her from above. Sue reached up one of her arms and found Remy's clit and began pulling on it as I was pinching on her nipples. Her eyes began to close in sheer ecstasy. I held on to Remy as she bent her knees and slid down on the strap-on that Sue was wearing, and told her, "Get on that dick and ride it real good, Remy." She didn't even flinch as it disappeared inside of her.

"Oh yeah. Mmm."

"Mmm hmmm," Remy and Sue moaned at the same time as Remy let the dildo slide in and out of her. Riding it as only a champion like herself could do.

As she was riding on the fake dick, Sue reached up and began pinching on Remy's nipples, making her ride it even harder. The men and I just stood there watching and enjoying the view of Remy's fat pussy coating the dildo with her essence. Remy was riding the dildo so hard that you could hear her and Sue's body making contact. We only watched for a couple more minutes before stopping them. Remy looked at me with a crazy gaze and asked, "What's the problem, Nikki?" She went up and down one more time and then continued, "This shit is getting good." She started up again, and Sue pushed up, meeting her thrust for thrust.

Remy looked up at me and as she did, her cum began to coat the strap-on. "Shit, I'm cumming," she said in her sexy voice.

It's now time for someone else to join in, and I saw John and Mark still stroking themselves. John left my side and kneeled down in the back of her and spread her ass cheeks as the dildo rested inside of her hot pussy. Mark walked over and stood in front of Remy as she welcomed him into her mouth. "Hell yeah," I said as I decided to join in on the fun and bend down to straddle Sue's face.

I looked over at Travis, who had just been sitting on the sidelines as Sue sucked my clit into her mouth, the folds of my pussy covering her face. I grabbed Travis' dick and sucked it into my mouth, letting a little of my saliva drip out of my mouth and onto Sue. As I heard John slam into Remy, it made me suck on Travis even harder, applying as much pressure as I could. "Suck that dick, Nikki," Travis said as Remy opened her eyes and stole a glance.

John pulled all the way out and slammed into her harder as she devoured Mark's dick. It made me happy to know that she was enjoying herself. I loved watching her suck dick, because she did it with such expertise. Mark grabbed a handful of her hair as he fucked her mouth, his balls hitting her chin as she reached and pinched her nipples really hard. John was slamming his dick in and out of her, and I could tell by the movement of her body that she was about to cum. I let go of Travis' dick and told her, "Cum, Remy. Squirt that shit out for me."

Mark was having a hard time keeping his dick in her mouth as her cum squirted out everywhere. She came so hard she couldn't control it like usual. Her body began to tense up, and I continued to watch her as I took Travis back into my mouth and Remy continued sucking Mark's dick. She sucked on it for only a few more minutes before he pulled it out, and as Remy lay back, he guided it into her pussy. He grabbed her legs and hoisted them over his shoulders so he could go deep. The sweat was dripping off of him onto her, and as his legs began to shake, he pulled out and came all over her stomach. She reached between her legs and pulled on her clit, making herself cum again. There was a sheen of sweat covering her body, causing it to glow in the dim lighting. Mark's cum slid down her body as I continued sucking Travis' dick until he exploded in my mouth. I swallowed every drop because the shit was just too good to waste.

Remy lay still as I stood up. Her chest heaving up and down as cum slid down her. Mark and John each grabbed one of Sue's legs and spread them apart. I reached my hand out and pulled Remy up from her position and asked, "You okay?"

She replied in her voice of innocence, "Yeah, I'm good. This is much better than where we were before."

I laughed to myself as I took the strap-on off of Sue and placed it around my own waist. Remy got even more excited as she spread her ass cheeks and squatted down over Sue's face, the cum still covering her. I could hear Sue's breathing quicken. I changed my mind and told Sue, "Get up on all fours. I wanna fuck you from the back."

Mark and John let go of her legs so she could turn over. Remy lay down on the blanket in front of her, and Sue buried her head in her pussy immediately. Remy reached her arms down and assisted Sue by spreading her lips farther apart. The feeling became intense as I watched Remy enjoy herself. I felt a tinge of jealousy as Sue sucked on her clit and then flicked her tongue over it really fast. I was wondering if Sue was making her feel as good as I did, or better. She licked from her pussy to her ass.

The men grabbed Remy's legs and held them up as they spread them apart, allowing Sue to get better access. Sue pushed her tongue hard into Remy's ass and then drug it along her folds. Remy's back arched and I could see her beginning to shake. She used her own fingers to pinch her nipples and then suddenly, "Oh my god. Yes. Yes, I'm fucking cumming. Shit."

Her back arched as Sue continued to suck on her clit. Remy was panting as she raised her head and at that same time, I slammed into Sue with the strap-on dick. I fucked her hard, as if she had committed a crime and this was her punishment. Remy and the guys watched as I pounded into Sue's pussy like a real man. Mark and John bent down and pulled on her hardened nipples. Sue moaned loud and told me she was about to cum. "Oh. Oh, yes. I'm about to cum. Don't stop."

I spread her ass cheeks again and rammed my thumb into her hole as she jerked back against me. Suddenly, her cum squirted out and drained down her thighs, making them shine. The dick around my hips was covered in pussy juice. I smiled at Remy as she smiled back at me.

Travis was ready to join in again and came behind me and entered me. He didn't waste any time as his hard dick moved in and out of me, causing me to shudder. John stood behind Remy, and she rose up on her tiptoes as he spread her ass cheeks and entered. "Oh, shit," she blurted out from the invasion.

She finally settled down flat footed as he worked the dick inside of her walls. She leaned back against him and brought her arms up and around his neck. He wrapped his arms around her, just below her breast line. Her rock-hard nipples stood at attention. I could see his dick working its magic between her legs, her pussy lips mashing down on top of it.

I smiled and looked over at Mark, who was off to the side stroking his own dick. He looked over at Sue and her wet pussy, as she looked up at him and then spread her legs, inviting him over. "Come on and get some of this wet pussy," she told him seductively.

She began rubbing her clit as he smiled and then dropped to his knees. He grabbed her legs roughly as he slammed his dick into her ready and willing pussy. Her body tensed up as he rubbed her clit through her puffy pussy lips. Remy was on the other side, moving her body to meet John's rhythm, looking as if she was really enjoying the dick inside of her. I then pushed my body back against Travis as it began to tremble. I reached over and grabbed the base of Mark's dick as it went in and out of Sue. Remy was watching me with envy in her big brown eyes as John fingered her nipples.

As her breasts bounced up and down on her chest, I could tell that she was about to cum. I watched as Mark pushed his dick into Sue a couple of more times and then pulled out, shooting his cum all on her stomach. He then dropped down and pulled her clit into his mouth, making her squirt her juices all over his bearded chin. Travis was darting in and out of me full force. I knew he was about to cum, so I pushed back, making him fall out of me, and then I turned around and caught all of his seeds. I felt his body tense up as his ass cheeks tightened. John picked up the pace and slammed into Remy harder. "Oh, shit," he yelled loudly as he pulled out of her and came all over her ass and back.

Remy came at the same time, her cream sliding down her thighs, coating them like lotion. I wanted Remy even more now and pulled her down to the blanket in front of me. I lifted one leg on each shoulder and then put the strap around my hips and pushed inside of her. Her eyes opened wide as she looked up at me smiling. Her pussy was taking every inch of the dildo as her body glistened with sweat, her chest heaving up and down. Travis reached down and began jacking her clit at the same time. I wanted to slow down and enjoy this, but I couldn't. The feeling was too intense. I thrust in and out of her endlessly. Her lips slightly parted, as if she wanted to say something, but no words came out. Suddenly, her cum covered the strap-on as she gripped the covers under her. I looked over and saw something I didn't see before. Sue was on all fours as John fucked her in the ass and Mark fucked her mouth.

I watched Remy's expression, and she lightly chuckled. As John went in and out of Sue, she reached down and began pulling on her own clit. John pulled all the way out and then slammed back into her roughly. Her body continuously shook. She was stroking herself faster and sucking Mark harder. I was amazed at her stamina as she began cumming. Mark and John both pulled out at the same time and covered her with cum. They were breathing hard but steady.

When they were finished, they all collapsed on the blanket under them, exhausted but completely satisfied. Remy closed her eyes and breathed lightly through her mouth, settling down. It had been one hell of a night for all of us. First, the BDSM party, and now this. We all just laid back for a while before getting up and cleaning ourselves up. We all said our goodbyes and made plans to do this again. Remy and I finally left to get some much-needed rest. I already knew I would be calling into work again. I needed to relax because the concert was this weekend, and anything was bound to happen.

Sugar E. Wallz

Chapter Fourteen

I had fallen into a deep sleep and suddenly, there he was, tall, dark, and sexy as fuck. His dreads pulled back by a single band. How dare he invade my dreams and take over. He reached up and caressed my face. His beautiful, smooth finger brushing against my bottom lip. I closed my eyes, almost melting from his touch. Butterflies formed in the pit of my stomach. Feelings unknown to me embracing my body and mind. These types of feelings were not allowed in my world. Who the fuck gave him permission to make me feel this way?

He came closer and removed his finger, replacing it with his perfectly formed tongue, tracing along the shape of my lips before pushing it into my mouth. His kiss was aggressive, almost bringing me to my knees. I was trying to pull away, but the dream wouldn't let me. Instead, it pulled me deeper.

He ran a thumb over my nipple and it instantly stood at attention. Chills began to cover my body as he slowly and seductively removed my top, exposing my bare breasts. I tried to speak to tell him no, but no words came out of my mouth. He bent down and pulled a nipple into his warm mouth, and as I tried to catch my breath, he stopped, looked me in the eyes, and grabbed my hand. He walked me to a bed I didn't even know was there. I pulled back, but his grip was too strong and he didn't let go. The room felt familiar, as if I had been there before. He lay me down on the bed and unbuttoned my jeans. He stared as he pulled them down over my thighs and then over my small feet. He dropped them to the floor beside us. I didn't know what was happening inside of me but I was so wet that I could feel my juices draining out of my pussy, forming a puddle beneath my ass on the silky sheets below.

I now watched him as he took off the clothing that was holding him hostage. His perfect form in front of me. His long, beautiful, black dick standing erect and waiting for me to embrace it. I couldn't fight against the feeling anymore and sat up. I stuck my tongue out and began licking around the head of his prized possession, and then I wrapped my hand around it. A hand almost too small to hold on to the beast in front of me. As I secured my grip, I opened my mouth wide and took him in. His pre-cum disappeared and absorbed my tongue as I sucked on him lightly. The quiet was broken by a deep moan from his lips. "Mmm mmm."

It sounded, like a sweet lullaby to my ears. His taste was so sweet, so different. I sucked on him harder and cupped his balls into my free hand. I massaged and pulled on them, as if I was picking apples that had ripened because they had grown on a good tree. Then, suddenly, he pushed me away and fell out of my mouth. I looked up at him, wondering and waiting. I felt like he was depriving me of what I now needed. He smiled, and it warmed my heart. He then bent down once again and attacked my lips with his sensual kiss. This time, more passionately. He gently pushed me back on the bed with his body and broke the kiss.

He looked me in the eyes before lifting off of me and lifted my legs, bending them at the knee and spreading them apart. My swollen clit peeked out, as if it's watching his every move. I suddenly felt his hot breath as it got closer to my pearl. My pussy opened to him as if he owned it. When his tongue flicked across my clit, I flinched and tried again to speak. Still, no words were forming. My pussy felt as if it's calling his name. A name that only it knew, one that was unfamiliar to me. It's almost as if he and my pussy shared a secret that I was not allowed in on.

I felt a finger slide inside of me as he sucked my stiffened clit. I wanted him to go faster and suck harder, but I couldn't get the words out to tell him. "Mmm, hmm." All I could do was moan and rotate my hips. I tried to thrust them hard, but he was the one in control of my body. All I could do was submit to him and his demands. His finger sped up. It was going into my wet hole faster, causing my heart to speed up and feel like it was about to beat out of my chest. He sucked on my clit harder as my legs began to tremble around him, and I knew that I couldn't hold it any longer.

"Aaah." I couldn't help but scream as my cum squirted out of me and all over those precious limbs he had inside of me. Steady, he continued to suck on me and cause me to go crazy. "Aaah, mmm." When I stopped cumming, he lifted his head and the sweet essence of my pussy was there on his wonderful lips, as if it was tattooed upon them.

I already knew how it tasted, so I knew exactly how he felt. He climbed further up me and was now hovering over me. As he attacked my nipple, pulling one at a time into his mouth, I couldn't help but embrace him. I felt his dick at the opening to my soul and slowly it invited him in. His dick opened me wide with its thickness. The pain was pleasurable and as I lifted my legs higher, I could feel him go even deeper. Slow and steady strokes in and out of me. This was not fucking that he was doing to me. No, he was making love to the pussy and I couldn't stop him. This felt too damn good and made me want more. I reached down and grabbed his ass cheeks and pulled him into me as his hips held a steady rhythm. I felt as if he was growing longer and wider as he threw his body into mine. I could feel his dick pulsing and wished that I could stop it, because I didn't ever want him to be finished. No, I wanted all of his seeds inside of me as if I was afraid he would share them with another. I dug my nails into him as he thrust into me one last time with extra aggression. He was trembling but not pulling out of me, as if he had read my mind.

Suddenly, I jerked awake and he was gone. I sat up in my bed and looked around my room as if I would really find him there, but he was not there. I caught an attitude because I was mad at myself for allowing him to invade my dreams. He's not supposed to be in my mind. I had to push him out but I was finding it hard to do. I didn't have room in my life for this man. I felt that he was trying to take something from me that I was not willing to give. My heart. I finally got out of my bed and went to the bathroom so I could take a shower. I somehow felt that I could wash him off of me, but I knew it was going to be impossible. I didn't have time to catch feelings for him, because I had better things to do.

Sugar E. Wallz

Chapter Fifteen

The weekend was finally here and the concert was being held tonight at the downtown arena. I was anxious because I needed the distraction to help me forget about the dream. My phone rang and it was Remy, trying to find out what time I was going to scoop her up. I told her the time and we continued to talk for a few minutes before hanging up. I was still trying to recover from my dream the night before. I brushed it off and continued on with my day. I spent the day spring cleaning my condo and the hours began to fly by. Before I knew it, it was time to go get Remy. I had plans to pick her up and bring her back here and who knows, maybe even get in a good fuck before we got dressed and left.

I got to her room and knocked, and she opened the door for me. "Hey, I've been waiting for you," she said in her melodic voice, and continued, "Girl, I am so ready to be surrounded by some fine niggas."

I shrugged my shoulders and said, "Yeah, Rem, me too. Maybe we can find us a little treat to share while we're there."

We left her room and returned to my place where her outfit had been since we bought it, so she didn't have to bring anything with her. When we walked in, Remy started stripping off all her clothes and, of course, I followed suit and told her, "Let's go hop in this shower and get ready."

She smiled and said nothing as she went into the bathroom. The water felt wonderful hitting my body and caused my nipples to stand at attention. I looked at Remy and stared at her perky breasts just sitting there perfectly, staring back at me. "What you looking at, Nikki?" she asked while looking at me seductively.

I wanted to chill but knew that this may be the perfect chance to help me get the dream out of my head and to forget about the sexy dread that was in it. As Remy was washing her face, I reached my hand over and pinched one of her nipples. I pinched and pulled at the same time. Remy opened her eyes and looked up at me while drawing her bottom lip into her mouth. I bent down and sucked one of her nipples into my mouth. I switched to the other one and continuously went back and forth. Remy then lifted one leg up and placed it on the side of the tub. As she did this, I reached a hand down and spread her pussy lips. "Yes, Nikki. Yes," she said hungrily as I pulled the hood back on her swollen bud.

I pressed down hard on it with my finger before dropping to my knees. As the water ran over our bodies, I sucked Remy's clit like a lollipop. "Mmm. God, yes. Suck it, Nikki." I had a small vibrator that I kept in the shower for those times I was alone. I reached over and grabbed it off the shower ledge, turned it on, and slid it into her. Remy gyrated her hips in a perfect circular motion, pushing her pussy into my face. She started to shake and said, "Oh my god, Nikki, I'm going to cum. Yes." I continued to fuck her with the vibrator as she came. I wanted her to get it all out. When I finally pulled it out, I continued to suck on her clit for a few more minutes. For some reason, this made me think of the dread in my dream. It actually intensified his presence. Remy's voice broke my daydream, "Come on, Nikki, let me suck that pussy and return the favor."

She put her hand between my pussy lips, but I just couldn't do it. For some reason, it didn't feel right. I pushed her hand away and said, "Nah Remy. I'm not feeling that right now." She looked at me with a confused look on her face but at that moment, I didn't give a fuck. I didn't belong to her and to me, she was just another fuck. Her feelings didn't mean shit to me.

We continued and finished our shower and then got out to dry off. The room was eerily quiet as we got dressed, and you could cut the tension in the air with a knife. She knew that something was off but didn't dare to question me. I wasn't going to let her ruin my night, because I had been looking forward to this concert and was going to have a good time whether she liked it or not.

I had ordered us a limo for tonight so we could show up in style. Who knows, I might just change my mind and let her sex me on the way. "Come on, the limo's outside," I told her. We gathered our purses and left the condo. Remy still had an attitude but at that moment, I really didn't care. She got in first and when I got in, I looked at her and she rolled her eyes. I just laughed it off and shook my head.

The limo was decked out with a mini bar, a TV, and even game consoles. Soft music was playing from the speakers and I settled into a relaxed mood. Sitting with my head leaned back and my eyes closed, I heard Remy ask me, "You want to drink something with me?"

I opened my eyes and smiled at her and took the drink she had prepared for me. The drink made me a little tipsy, and I turned to look at Remy, who was also looking at me with a deep hunger in her eyes and a sly smile across her lips. She got up and crawled over to me like a cat on the prowl. The Versace bodysuit I had on had a zipper that ran from my breasts all the way down to my pussy. Remy never broke eye contact as she unzipped the body suit, freeing my breasts and exposing my pussy to her watering mouth. She took my phone out of my hand and sat it to the side, and then went down between my thighs, pulling my clit into her mouth. When she pushed a finger into me, I could tell she still had an attitude from the force of it. I looked up and could see the driver watching us through the rearview mirror. It turned me on even more, and I winked at him. I whispered to Remy, "Let's give the driver a show."

I then grabbed the back of her head and ground my hips really hard, smothering her with my pussy. She had on a short skirt, so while she was sucking my pussy, I reached down and pulled it up, knowing she didn't have any panties on. I felt the limo suddenly swerve a little and giggled. I mouthed for him to pull over and when he did, Remy lifted her head up, wondering what was happening. I looked at her and shook my head while pushing her head back where it belonged.

The limo driver didn't get out and walk to the back door to get in, but instead, crawled through the middle window to join us. He was a sexy black brother with waves and a small goatee that could tickle my ass while he ate my pussy. But tonight, I was gonna let him get some of Remy's good pussy.

She looked up at me and then back at the limo driver, and smiled when she realized what was about to happen. She then went back where she belonged, between my thighs. The limo driver pulled his dick out and spanked Remy on the ass with his hardness. His dick was long and smooth, and I was kinda jealous that it was going in Remy instead. Her pussy was already filled with wetness, so he slid into her with ease. I looked up at him and said, "You better fuck her good."

He nodded his head and smiled, and then pounded into her. Remy began sucking my clit even harder, bringing me close to my orgasm. "Oh my god, Remy. I'm about to cum."

As I told Remy that, he fucked her even harder and faster, and as my cum squirted out on her chin, he pulled out and shot all between her ass cheeks. We all laughed together and then started getting cleaned up. When we were done, the limo driver climbed back up into the front seat, started the limo, and then winked at me through the rearview mirror before pulling off, driving us to our destination.

Chapter Sixteen

We finally made it to the arena where the concert was being held. The parking lot was packed. The groupies everywhere were scream- ing and jumping up and down, hoping for an opportunity with the rappers. Remy and I had backstage passes, so we knew our time would come soon enough. We looked at the groupies and then each other, and said at the same time, "Thirsty hoes."

When we got to the entrance, the bouncer looked us up and down and licked his lips lustfully. Remy tiptoed up against his tall frame and whispered something in his ear. If I knew her like I thought I did, we would be sucking his dick and swallowing his seed very soon. We were escorted inside by a big butch looking female and taken to the front of the arena right below the stage. These spots were the best in the house and cost a pretty penny but were well worth it. Remy looked at me and said, "Thanks for inviting me." I shrugged my shoulders and smiled at her, letting her know I appre- ciated the gesture.

The music got really loud, and then the crowd started cheering. I turned and saw a sexy dread enter the stage. I suddenly noticed that it was the dread I'd been trying to avoid, the same one from my dream, and I wanted to run away. I tried so hard to look away so he didn't see me, but my eyes just wouldn't let me. I could feel Remy nudging me, but I couldn't break my stare, and that was when he noticed me and stopped speaking to the crowd.

The crowd was silent and curious as to why he stopped talking. The crowd waited, but he seemed to be at a loss for words. A few minutes passed, and he said, "Sorry about that, but I got mesmerized when I laid my eyes on an angel." I almost fainted right then and there and could have sworn the whole crowd was looking at me. Then I heard him continue, "There is a beautiful woman here to- night, and I just lost my composure." I was embarrassed yet flattered at the same time. I turned around to walk away, telling Remy I'd be back, but she chose to follow anyway. She wanted to find the bouncer that had let us in.

As soon as I turned a corner, I bumped right into the dread. I looked at Remy, hoping to distract myself, but I noticed that she was walking away with the bouncer. I was on my own now. I could feel my pussy get wet instantly as my knees began to grow weak. He held his hand out for me to shake and introduced himself, "Hey, I'm Robert." I tried to tell him my name, but my lips wouldn't move. "You're Nicole, right?"

I didn't know how he knew my name and was stunned when he said it. He smiled and started to speak, but I cut him off, "Umm yeah, uh, look, I have to go find my friend."

He shot back, "Can I get your number before you disappear again?" Something took over me and I started giving him the digits. I didn't ever give random niggas my number, so I didn't know what the fuck I was thinking. However, it was too late to take it back.

I turned and left him standing there, determined to curse Remy's ass out for leaving me. I walked into the women's restroom and heard familiar moaning coming from the back stall. I went to investigate and opened the door to find Remy getting dicked down. The bouncer had her against the wall. She turned to me and said, "Girl, this dick is good."

Her legs were wrapped around his waist, and he was fucking her so hard I swore I could feel it. That nigga's nuts were hanging low and I reached out and said, "What the fuck. I might as well."

I cupped his balls in my hand and pulled on them as he pounded into her. As I took my other hand and ran a finger up and down his ass crack, his look changed, and I knew he was about to cum. "Oh, shit. I'm cumming."

He pulled out of Remy and shot his cum all over the stalls walls. His dick was enormous, and I couldn't believe that she took all of it. He seemed to really like her and when they were done, they exchanged numbers. After he left, Remy giggled and said, "Girl, did you see the size of that dick?"

I responded, "Yeah, bitch. That shit was an anaconda. Your pussy probably stretched big as the ocean now."

We laughed and continued on back to our spots at the front of the stage. The "Money Boyz" had graced the stage and had the crowd hyped up by the time we got back. Their music was really fly, and I couldn't wait to go backstage and meet them. The whole concert lasted about two and a half hours and when it was over, we utilized our backstage passes.

We met all three of the rappers and they invited us to an after party they were having back at their hotel, and we told them we'd be happy to go. They told us the location and we left. We went back to my place first so we could take a shower and change clothes, and then we headed to the hotel where the real party would begin. When we got to the hotel, one of the rappers greeted us in the lobby. He walked us upstairs to their room where there were drinks and pills all over the table. One of them was smoking a blunt, and Remy pulled it out of his hand to take a pull. Everyone was sitting around chilling and feeling good. It was only me, Remy, and the three rappers. She was flirting hard with the men, but my mind was somewhere else.

I began daydreaming about Robert and imagined greeting him after he came home from a long day of work. His dinner cooked and waiting for him to devour it. As he walked in the front door, I'd greet him with a sensual kiss, just big enough to show him he was missed. I grabbed his coat and went to hang it up as he removed his shoes. I prepared him a hot bath while he's eating, just hot enough to soothe his aching muscles.

After he finished his meal, he walked into the bathroom and began to undress. I stood up and turned to help him. I unbuttoned his shirt and pulled it down from his chiseled arms and back. I pulled his wife-beater over his head, revealing his cut chest. His dark-brown skin glowing under the brightness of the bathroom light. I then went to his waist and unbuttoned his jeans. I slid them down and over his feet as he lifted up one leg at a time. Before I stood, I looked and saw the head of his dick poking out from the slit in his boxers. I couldn't help but giggle because I'm flattered that my touch alone did this to him. I pulled his boxers down next and his erect dick was staring at me.

Robert got in the tub and leaned back. His head was against the wall pillow. I looked at him completely submerged in the water and my pussy became wet. I dropped my robe and stood there completely naked while looking at him. My nipples erect and my clit swollen and peeking out of my pussy lips. I reached my hands to my breasts and pulled on my nipples before pushing up one breast to my lips, and then stuck my tongue out to lick it while looking deep into his eyes. I stuck one foot in the hot water and then the other, keeping my legs slightly spread. He reached his hand up between my legs and slipped a finger into my pussy. I began to rotate my hips against his hand like he had a real dick inside of me. His finger was glistening from my juice. You could hear the sounds of my creamy pussy as he pulled his finger in and out.

His finger was no longer enough for me, so I reached down and pulled his hand from between my thighs. I looked down at his massive dick and then squatted down onto it. It felt like it was splitting me open as it slowly disappeared inside of me. I grabbed onto the sides of the tub to steady myself and ride the dick inside of me. Robert began to play with my nipples as I gently went up and down on his shaft. "Oh, mmm." I was moaning in pleasure as the water splashed onto his brown skin. I began to ride him faster, his shaft rubbing against my clit with each stroke, making it tingle. "I'm about to cum all over this dick. Oh yeah." I was at my peak now as I told him I was about to cum. I wanted him to cum with me, so I squeezed my pussy muscles really tight. I told him in between moans, "Mmm. Cum, mmm hmm, cum with me. Mmm." As my cum began to coat his dick, he grabbed my thighs really tight and pushed up, slamming into me. His seeds filled my insides and my walls soaked up all of his essence.

"Nicole. Nicole. Damn, girl, can you hear me?" I was snapped out of my daydream by Remy's voice and noticed that I was still in the hotel. I was breathing heavily and looking around the room for Robert, but he was not there. Remy and the guys were already naked and looking at me crazy and saying, "Hey. We waiting on you."

My mind couldn't comprehend anything right now, so I stood up and said, "I got to go to the bathroom. Go ahead and start without me." I already knew that Remy could handle these men by herself, so I went to the bathroom and left her there to do so. I shut the door and ran the cold water for a couple of seconds before splashing some on my face. I then looked in the mirror and said to my reflection, "I can do this."

I dried my face and then walked back out into the room, ready to join Remy and the guys for a good time. When I walked in, all eyes were on me, and I saw Remy smiling. She got up and grabbed my hand, and we walked over and stood in front of the mirror. We began dancing seductively and kissing each other. The men all sat back, watching us, their hardened dicks in their hands.

Remy pinched my nipples as I reached around and grabbed her ass cheeks, squeezing them and then spreading them to expose her asshole. I sat down on the dresser and lifted my legs as Remy dropped to her knees. She was kissing and caressing my body as the guys sat still and watched the show. I knew they were ready to fuck, but we gave them strict orders that we were running the show, and they couldn't move until we said so. I felt one of her small, slender fingers slide inside of me and as I leaned my head back, a moan escaped my lips. "Mmm, Remy."

She then inserted another one and went as deep as her fingers would let her. My pussy was drenched as she pulled my clit into her mouth and softly sucked it. I rotated my hips to the motion of her tongue. She was flicking it over my clit while fucking me with her fingers at the same time. "Oh yes, Remy. Yes, baby." I knew the men were tired of waiting, so I gently pushed her from between my legs and nodded my head towards the men. She understood and rose to her feet. I got up off the dresser and grabbed her hand as we walked to the bed together. The three men lay in the bed side by side. I mounted the one on the left and began to turn sideways but changed my mind. I came up off of him and told him, "I want you to hit this pussy from the back."

Remy got to the nigga on the right side while the third man stayed in the middle of the bed. She and I got on all fours and faced each other, the third nigga's dick in the middle of our faces. We both grabbed one nut each as the niggas in the back of us spread our ass cheeks. As their dicks slid into us, we stuck out our tongues and

flicked them over the middle man's dick. We then took turns sucking the head of him into our mouths. He tasted sweet, as if he had
bathed in fruity body wash. The thought of his clean dick enticed
me to pull a ball in between my lips and suck.

The guy behind me was slamming into me hard as I stuck a
finger up the middle man's ass. He flinched and looked down at me
crazy but didn't bother to protest. I knew that a lot of niggas secretly
liked that shit, they just didn't want to admit it. The dude behind
Remy was slamming into her so hard that she couldn't hold on to
the middle man's dick any longer and let it go. Their bodies made a
clapping noise, but you could faintly hear her sticky wetness as he
went in and out of her. He suddenly stiffened and then pulled out of
her, shooting his seeds all over her ass.

When he pulled out, she got on the bed and mounted the mid-
dleman backwards and began riding his dick. Her breasts bounced
up and down as I reached over and played with her clit. The nigga
behind me finally pulled out and came all over my back. Remy's
cum covered the middle man's dick now, and as he pushed her up
off of him and shot his cum high, my pussy began to flow. We finished and all lay back, sweating and trying to gain control of our
breath.

The group told us about a tour they were about to start and asked
Remy and I to go. I knew this could be a great opportunity, at least
for Remy, so I said I'd think about it and get back to them. Maybe
if I went I could forget about Robert, and I was willing to do anything to forget about him.

Chapter Seventeen

When Remy and I left the hotel, I took her straight home. She was hoping to come home with me, but I needed some alone time. When I walked into my condo, I dropped everything at the front door and walked straight to the couch. I didn't even get undressed before laying down on the couch and falling asleep. I didn't know how long I had been asleep for when I heard my cell phone ring, waking me from my slumber. I answered without even looking to see who it was, and I felt my heart skip a beat as soon as I heard his voice. "Hey, Nicole. This is Robert. I just wanted to check on you."

I spoke back in a stutter. "I-I-I-I'm good. Wh-what's up?" I was excited and nervous all at the same time. We talked for hours and got to know each other. I really enjoyed myself too. We made plans to hook up the following weekend, which was when The Money Boyz would start their tour. I hated to do it, but I would have to tell Remy she was on her own. I couldn't turn Robert down even if I wanted to.

As soon as I hung up, my phone rang again, and it just so happened to be my boss, Jamal, telling me he needed me to come into the office the next day because he needed my help writing out a very important proposal for a new investor. Although it was still the weekend, I told him that I would be there. I had already missed a few days of work, so I knew I should show my face.

I took a long, hot, much-needed shower and laid down. Trying to sleep was hard because I couldn't get Robert out of my mind. I suddenly became wet and knew what I needed to do. I had a full-length mirror hung on my wall and went and got a chair to sit in front of it. I started off by admiring my curves, and then ran my hands from my nipple to my pussy. I stopped and walked over to my nightstand and pulled out my dildo. I then sat down in front of the mirror and pulled my legs up and opened so I could see my pussy. I opened my pussy lips and watched myself play with my clit. I looked myself in the eyes and smiled, because I knew I was a nasty bitch. This pussy belonged to me, and I could do whatever the fuck I wanted to do with it. I took the dildo and slowly slid it inside of me. I watched as my pussy hole sucked it right in and almost swallowed it. "Ssss. Yes."

I pushed it in and out slowly as my creamy juices coated it. I stopped and without pulling it out, I got up and slid my chair closer to the mirror. I then sat back down and continued fucking myself. My clit was fat and swollen, looking like it was about to pop. The dildo filled me like a real dick and made me moan like a man was on top of me. "Yes. This shit feels so good. Mmm." I could feel myself getting ready to cum, so I worked the dildo faster, my fat pussy holding on to it like a hostage. "Fuck. I'm cumming. I'm cumming." My cum squirted all over the dildo and my hand, but I continued until nothing was left. I was covered in sweat, and when I put my legs down to stand, I felt weak. The orgasm was intense, and it took me a minute to catch my breath. I didn't even have the strength to take another shower, so I got in my bed, wet pussy and all, and drifted off to sleep.

When my alarm went off and woke me up the next morning, it felt like I had just gone to sleep. I couldn't even do my routine cumming session because I was so exhausted from the night before. I usually didn't let anything come between me and my morning orgasm, but I just didn't have the strength to pull through.

I got to the office and walked in, ready to handle what Jamal needed handled, but found the place empty. I found that strange since he called me and asked me to come in. I decided I would wait a little while to see if he showed. I didn't know anything about a new client proposal, but I always tried to be there when Jamal needed me. I figured I could catch up on some other work while I was waiting for him. As soon as I turned my computer on, Jamal walked in. He had his shirt unbuttoned with his brown, chiseled chest staring directly at me. When he made it to my desk, he began unbuttoning his jeans. I thought we were there to work, so I asked, "Mr. Jackson, I thought we were going to be working on a proposal. What's up?"

He responded, "Yeah, Nicole, I want your mouth to propose to this dick." Now I was always down for some dick, but this was unexpected. After he undid his jeans, he pulled his dick out and began stroking it, and stated hungrily, "Why don't you let that pussy write a report all over my dick."

He then pulled me up from the chair and breathed heavily as his mouth met mine. He took my arms and placed them around his neck, over his shoulders, and looked me in the eyes. I pushed my body into his, as if I was melting into him, and surrendered my tongue once again. Inhaling his masculine aroma made me feel as if I was high off some potent drugs. He was kissing me hard, and I couldn't pull away even if I tried. He smelled so fresh and tasted so sweet as I was taking him all in. Our lips and tongues moved as if they were in the middle of a well-rehearsed dance. I was feeling like knots were twisting in my stomach, and my mind felt confused trying to sort out everything it was feeling.

He pulled up my skirt and grabbed my ass cheeks, caressing them roughly. His erect dick poking out and rubbing against my now exposed thighs. My legs slightly opened, as if getting ready for the size of him. His strong brown arm holding me captive was only adding to the gratification coursing through my body. I'd never felt so wanted and needed, and that alone was alien to me. I wanted to let go, but I couldn't escape him. He was a lot to take in. It was like this moment was my destiny.

He picked me up lightly, as if I would break, and turned me around to sit me on my desk. My pussy was wet and ready to receive him. "Oh, Jamal. I'm so fucking wet," I told him between breaths.

He looked at me and stated, "That was my intention." He then pushed into me with great force and then slowly pulled out, leaving only the head of his dick inside of me. My creamy juices left a thick shimmer on his length. He pushed back into me, causing a loud thud between our bodies. "Uugh." It was a hard thrust, but it felt wonderful, the heat it was emitting. Who the fuck invented this shit? There was nothing on the planet that compared to it.

He pulled all the way out and said with authority in his voice, "Turn over," and, of course, I submitted to his demands. My stomach was on the desk and sticking from the sweat it was permeating. He opened me up yet again and pushed into me harder, as if he had a grudge against me. I wanted to call out to him, but I had somehow lost my voice and couldn't, yet, I wouldn't give up searching for it. Who gave Jamal the right to make me feel this good?

Our bodies were slapping together even harder now, and I could feel my juices sliding down to my ass crack, and then it came back to me, my voice from the depths of my soul, and I called his name, "Oh, Robert."

Jamal suddenly stopped and looked at me and asked, "Who the fuck is Robert and why the fuck you calling me his name?"

I wasn't Jamal's bitch, so he had no right to question me about shit, but I played stupid and asked, "What the fuck are you talking about, Jamal?"

He replied, "Bitch, you just called me another nigga's name while I was deep in the pussy, that's what." This shit was crazy, and there was nothing I could say or do to save myself. Jamal pulled away and started putting his clothes back on and said, "Maybe you should take some time off, because it seems like you need to get yourself together."

He then walked away from me and walked out the door, slamming it while I still sat here with my skirt up and my pussy still wet and thinking about the nigga that consumed me.

Chapter Eighteen

I was still horny from my time with Jamal, so before leaving the office, I played with myself until I got the nut Jamal deprived me of. I decided that I should call Remy and tell her that I couldn't go with her and The Money Boyz. I figured I would lie and tell her I was going to be busy preparing a big presentation for a new client who could only make it to town that same weekend. I couldn't tell her about Robert. At least not yet. I knew that Remy felt something for me, and since I wasn't sure where things were headed with Robert just yet, I felt it was best to spare her feelings for now.

When I called, she asked me to come to her place, and I told her that I would be there within the hour. Fuck it. I might as well go have some more fun and just tell her in person. When I pulled up to the room Remy was staying at, I knocked, but it wasn't her that answered. It was a white girl with short cropped hair. "Hey, you must be Nikki," she said with a smile.

At first sight, you would have thought it was a boy, but the breasts gave her away. "Yes, I am Nikki," I said back as I looked down and saw the head of a pink strap-on peeking out from her blue robe.

She pulled the door open further as Remy walked up behind her. Remy was completely naked, her swollen clit poking out between her pussy lips. She grabbed onto the girl's arm and said, "Come on, Nikki. I got us a little treat." She then reached up and exposed the white girl's breast and twisted her nipple between her fingers. She stopped after a few seconds and reached her hand out to me, pulling me inside. As soon as she shut the door, she came up closer to me and began pulling on my clothes, telling me, "Take it off, Nikki. I got a no clothing policy here."

I couldn't even resist her little freaky ass, so I started undressing. As soon as I was naked, Remy sucked one of my nipples between her lips, and the white girl came over and started sucking the other. My clit was swollen and painfully pulsing. I felt the white girl's hand slide between my ass cheeks and find my pussy hole. My legs slightly spread and a sticky wetness formed between them.

Remy's long, pink tongue flicked over my nipple as a cool breeze blew against the wetness from her mouth, making me shake. I reached down to feel on Remy. Her territory usually felt familiar to my hands, but today, it was alien.

The white girl pushed a finger inside of me and gently guided it in and out. "Shit." She bent down and licked the entire length of my ass crack and then pulled her finger out of my pussy, guiding it to my asshole. She did it gently, as if she would hurt me. Remy went down on her knees in front of me and sucked my clit from the inside of my folds. I found myself trembling from the invasion. The two at the same time had me feeling drunk with pleasure. "Oh my god, yes. This shit feels so good." My eyes were closed, my mouth slightly open. A moan escaped me. "Mmm, Mmm." I felt as if I was about to faint, so I grabbed Remy for balance. I could feel myself about to explode and pulled her hair, clenching it in my fists really hard. "I'm cumming, Remy. Shit, I'm fucking cumming," I screamed out as my cum coated Remy's mouth and chin. Her lips looked as if they were coated with her own personal lip gloss. My hips rotated against the white girl, who now had the tip of her tongue on my asshole, licking it. When she stopped, I almost fell over. They both had to wrap their arms around me and hold me up.

Once I gained my composure, Remy went into another room and returned with a really thick comforter and laid it on the floor. She spread it out and told me, "Lay down, Nik. We ain't through with you yet." I was still dizzy from my orgasm, and it felt like I was recovering from a massive hangover. My was pussy throbbing, my nipples hard and sticking out.

I lie down and Remy squatted over my face. Her pussy scent invaded my nostrils and smelled like sweet honey. I felt the white girl spread my legs and then press down on my clit. She then slapped it, as if it had violated some kind of rule and needed punishment. The sensation felt good, but the stinging it left behind made it a little numb. Remy was playing with her clit over my face as I was looking at it. I stuck my log tongue out and licked her crack as far as I could reach. When she removed her finger, I replaced it with my tongue.

The white girl, still wearing the pink dildo that looked to be about eight inches, rubbed it the length of me before pushing the head in. My pussy wet with self-lubrication invited her. "How do you want it?" she asked, and I responded between licks on Remy's clit, "Long…hard…and very…very deep."

The sound of my cum squishing against the fake dick sounded nasty and oh, so good. She fucked me like an angry man, and I loved it. The harder she fucked me, the harder I sucked on Remy's clit. My cum built again and I knew Remy was ready too. The white girl pushed my legs up to my shoulders and dicked me down like a pro. I wasn't sure that she could go any deeper. "I'm cumming, Nikki. Suck it, baby. Suck it," Remy screamed as her sweet juice went down the side of my face, leaving a trail in its wake.

I reached down and played with my clit as the dick went in and out. The white girl slowed down as I told her, "I'm about to cum all over this dick." I came all over her pink strap-on and when she pulled out, my pussy was still throbbing. She waited a minute and then removed her strap-on and placed it around my hips as I lay there. I looked at her curiously, wondering whose pussy would get it next.

The white girl stood up and then over me and then squatted down on the dick. She reached her hands up to my breasts and latched onto them, as if he needed support. I then saw Remy come behind her with a small yellow dildo in her hand and knew what was about to happen. As she rode the dick attached to me, Remy slid the other dildo into my ass. Both of us getting fucked at the same time was intoxicating, so it wasn't a surprise when we both came at the same time.

Afterward, we all three just lay there for a while. When I finally awoke, I saw Remy on the couch spread eagled while the white girl was between her legs feasting. I didn't know where he came from, but there was a male behind the white girl, pounding into her hard. I didn't want to disturb their groove, so I just chilled until they were done. When they finished, I then got up and got dressed. Remy no-ticed me and jumped up off the couch, begging me to stay, but my ass was tired and worn out, so I told her I couldn't. I needed some time to myself anyway.

She walked me to the door but naked, with her nipples still poking out. I finally told her, "Remy, I'm not going to be able to go with you and the boys on tour. I'm sorry." I felt really bad, but I would make it up to her one day.

She looked at me with a sad expression and said, "It's okay, Nik. I can take care of them all by myself."

I laughed out loud and shook my head. Remy promised to bring me back some souvenirs from the different cities they visited. She would be gone for two long weeks, and I knew I would miss her like crazy. She had become my best friend and I knew I'd be lost without her. We agreed to hook up as soon as she got back, and I made her promise to ride the dick extra good and extra long just for me. I knew that she would be fine, but I wondered how I would be.

Chapter Nineteen

No sooner than I got in my car, my cell phone started ringing. I didn't even bother to look at the caller ID but just answered instead. At that present moment, I didn't even care who it was. As soon as I heard the deep voice on the other end, the butterflies began to fly around in my stomach. I didn't understand how this nigga had this effect on me. I hadn't even touched his lips except in my dreams, and I was already hooked. Robert asked me to meet him for dinner, and although I really wanted to just go home and get some rest, I couldn't tell him no. I gave him the directions to my place and then hung up and asked myself, "What the fuck did I just do?"

When I got to my condo, I sat in my car for a minute thinking about Robert and wondering what I would do with this situation I had created. I was feeling things I had never felt before. Things I didn't want to feel, but also things that I couldn't prevent. I finally got out of the car and went inside to prepare myself for what lay ahead. I only had about two hours before Robert would show up.

I removed my clothes and threw them into the washing machine because they felt extra dirty to me. However, it could have just been my conscience, because for some reason, I felt guilty about all my little rendezvous from the day. I somehow felt like I had cheated on him, and he wasn't even my man. I was feeling a little tense, so instead of a shower, I ran a bath. I just wanted to relax for a little bit. I remembered the last time Robert invaded my mind. My dreams possessed him and wouldn't let him go. I soaped up my bath sponge and began gliding it over my bare skin. When I ran the soapy sponge over my right nipple, I could feel my clit pulsate. I could see Robert in my vision as I pulled his bottom lip into my mouth, devouring it as if it were a piece of cake. His tongue darted out of his mouth and he ran it over my lips and then whispered in my ear, "This pussy belongs to me, and I'm about to put my mark on it."

He ran his fingers over my hardened nipples one by one. Chill bumps covered my body, and I was lost in his touch. My nipples painfully ached from their stiffness, and my breathing accelerated as his plump lips found them and ran over them like a bump in the road. He sucked and licked them hungrily as I called his name, "Oh, Robert. Yes, Robert."

I arched my back from the sensation as he switched from nipple to nipple, biting them with those straight white teeth. My clit throbbed, about to burst from the pressure, wanting this same mouth to explore its essence. It's as if he could hear my clit calling his name as he traveled lower until he reached it. I was trying to scream his name again, but as always, I had lost the ability to speak. I lost all senses when he was around me. All but my sense of touch. He was now pulling on my clit with his teeth, and I had to grab the sides of the tub to keep myself from going crazy. I wanted to reach down and push him into me harder, until he got lost in my folds. I finally let go of the tub and immersed my fingers into his dreads, holding them hostage so he couldn't escape me. My pussy was wet, not from the water but from the juices inside of me. I felt his fingers enter me and explore, as if they were searching for treasure. I pulled in a deep breath, and then he—

I jumped up and opened my eyes at the sound of the doorbell. Water splashed all over the floor as my heart felt like it was about to beat out of my chest. I got up and grabbed my robe, not even bothering to dry off. The time seemed to have flown by, and as I looked at the clock, I knew that it was him. I was nervous and hesitated and wondered what would happen if I didn't answer. But he was insistent and continued to ring the bell. My hair was in a towel, no shoes were on my wet feet, and a short, silky robe covered my nakedness, but I walked to the door anyway and turned the knob.

As soon as his presence enveloped me, the butterflies began their dance. "Damn it," I say it out loud, unintentionally, because these butterflies wouldn't go away.

"Are you okay?" he asked as he stood there looking like some sort of black god in front of me. My heart felt as if it was going into cardiac arrest as I just stood there and stared. How did he have the power to do this to me? I was paralyzed as he took me out of my trance by calling my name with those beautiful lips. "Nicole. Nicole. You straight?"

His eyes scanned me as he stood there with his aroma violating my nose. He was wearing all white, except for a black belt and black Timbs. The white jeans and t-shirt made his dark skin glow, and I just wanted to reach out and touch him, but I didn't, because with him, I wanted to be different. I finally told him, "I'm sorry. Please, come in."

His t-shirt defined the cuts in his chest. His small man nipples slightly poked out and made my mouth water. I was looking a mess, and yet, he was staring at me as if I was the most beautiful woman he had ever seen. He always made me feel that way and yet, he still told me, "You have got to be the most beautiful woman I've ever seen."

I blushed and told him, "Thank you." I paused, remembering what I had on, and then continued, "I'm so sorry. I just got out of the tub. Get comfortable while I go get dressed." I was so embarrassed as I left him standing there so I could make myself decent.

By the time I prepared myself for the night and went back to the living room, he told me, "Uhm. I went ahead and ordered us something to eat in. I hope that's okay."

I responded, "Damn, did I take that long?"

We giggled together and he was so intoxicating. I paid attention to all the details when it came to him. We decided to watch a movie off of Netflix and chill after we ate. It was already getting late. I wanted to stop the clock because I never wanted this time to end. I sat on the opposite end of the couch, although I really just wanted to sit on his dick. My mind was telling me to get closer when I heard him ask, "Why you so far away? Acting like you scared of a nigga and shit."

He opened his arms and I moved over closer to him, nudging myself under the arm he had propped up on the back of the couch. I then lay my head on his chest. The words were out of my mouth before I could stop them. "This feels good."

He moved a hand to my head and ran his fingers through my hair and said back to me, "Yeah. This feels better than good. This feels perfect."

Sugar E. Wallz

I opened my eyes to a bright light and realized it was the sun peeking through my window. I began to wonder as I looked around, was it real or was it all just a dream again? Then I saw it, a note on my coffee table signed by Robert, telling me that he would call me later. It was real. I was really in his arms. I must have been so comfortable that I fell asleep in the softest place on earth, his embrace.

I had never been in a man's arms that I wasn't fucking, so this was new to me. I wondered why he didn't try to fuck me like all the other men I knew and met, but I already knew why. Robert was different. I could feel it, and I knew he would be the one man who would change my life forever. I wondered if I was ready for that change. The mere thought of him had my body longing for his touch. This was a real man, and now that he was in my life, no other one would do.

Chapter Twenty

I got up and got myself together and decided to go into the office. I drove all the way there with Robert deep in my thoughts. I wondered exactly where this little thing we had was going. When I got to the office, I was told that Jamal was out of town for the next couple of days, but there were instructions on my desk for what he needed me to do, since he wasn't there. I decided not to stay. I left and went to get me some breakfast, this nigga still in my thoughts.

I decided that I would take Remy something to eat and spend some time with her before she left this weekend. I was so happy for her because this trip could bring her lots of possibilities. I was definitely going to miss her. That night I first saw her in the strip club, I knew she was the right bitch for me. She had turned into the friend that I had needed all my life. Me and females didn't click too well on a friendship level, because they would always have so much to say about or try to bring you down. All the other bitches I knew talked shit behind my back and told everything I said or did. Remy was a ride or die bitch and kept everything to herself. We could fuck a football team and no one would ever know but us and them. Remy was my bitch.

When I got to her room, I knocked but didn't get an answer. However, when I tried the knob, the door opened right up. I walked in and called her name but didn't get an answer. I heard the shower going, so I walked into the bathroom and pulled the curtain back. There was Remy in her beautiful brown skin. Small drops of water hung onto her long lashes. The water falling over her breasts and nipples looked like gemstones in the middle of a waterfall. I bit into my bottom lip, remembering the taste of her. I wanted her so bad at that very moment. She still had not sensed my presence, so I got undressed, never taking my eyes off of her. I eased in behind her and wrapped her in my embrace. She jumped and turned her head around, but after realizing it was me, she turned back around. Her breathing sped up from my touch, and as I kissed her neck, I could feel her body quiver, as if my kisses gave her chills.

She turned around to face me and said, "Glad you could join me," and then her lips met mine and we got lost in a slow, sensual kiss.

Our tongues intertwined as if in battle. We stopped for a brief second, and I traced the lines of her lips with my tongue and told her, "It's my pleasure, always my pleasure."

We kissed again, with more passion this time. I opened my eyes slightly and peeked down at her breasts. Her nipples were calling for me, so I pulled from her mouth and pulled one between my lips. The water brushed against my head, and it sounded like a sweet melody to my ears, a slow jam playing in my mind. I gently bit each nipple and heard her moaning, "Oh. Oh, yes."

I bit even harder because I didn't want her to forget my touch while she was on that tour bus with all those men. When she was riding a dick, I wanted her to think about the sweet taste of my pussy. I needed to give her something to think about.

She grabbed a handful of my hair and locked her fingers up in it. I took a hand down to her pussy and pressed it against her clit. I pressed really hard and moved them in a circular motion at the same time as she called out to me, "Oh, Nik. I'm gonna fucking miss this shit." It felt as if she was about to pull my hair out as I felt my hand become wet. This wetness was not from the shower water but from the walls of her pussy. I wanted to taste her, so I pushed her gently back against the wall, and now the force of the water was beating down against my back. "Come on, Nikki, stop playing."

She was pushing hard on my head, trying to force me down, but I was taking my time. I didn't want to look over any spot on her body. I knew my way around every crevice. I knew what she needed because it was what I needed too. I wanted her cum on my lips, my chin, and the tip of my tongue. I could feel her balance herself as I rolled my tongue over her clit. I knew it wasn't going to take her long to cum, and I wouldn't make her wait because I wanted my turn too.

I stuck two fingers inside of her, and her pussy embraced them like a warm hug. I located her G-spot inside and hit it as much as I could. Remy tightened her muscles, holding my fingers captive. She was becoming wetter, and my pussy followed suit and became drenched. Her pussy tasted so good I wanted to savor the flavor. As she ground her hips into my mouth, I pulled my fingers in and out as I sucked her clit harder. Her body stiffened, and she said, "Make me cum, Nikki. Make this pussy cum." As her essence erupted onto my fingers, she called my name, "Nikki. Fuck. Bitch, I'm cum-ming."

My name sounded different coming from her lips. I licked her hole, trying to catch all of her, and when she was done, I told her, "I'm going to miss this good pussy."

We shared a laugh and then finished taking a shower. When we were done, we went to the bedroom dripping wet, so Remy could give me what I needed to last me the next two weeks.

We left a trail of water as we walked to the bed, and I climbed up as Remy left the room, telling me she needed to get something from the other room, wondering what she was going to get. My mind drifted to Robert, and I was curious as to what he was doing at that very moment. Was he sucking a bitch's pussy like me? The thought of it pissed me off and at about that time, Remy walked in with a cup of ice and a big black dildo. She sat both on the bedside table and then spread my legs apart. My clit was already swollen from the thoughts I held in my head. She said nothing as she reached down and pulled on my clit so hard it felt as if she was ripping it off. The sudden pain brought me a tiny bit of pleasure. She then reached over and grabbed the cup of ice and said to me, "I'ma fuck you real good today, Nikki."

She took an ice cube and pushed it into me. It was really cold, but the heat from my insides was making it melt quickly. The cold-ness poured out of me and ran down the crack of my ass. She bent over and lapped the liquid from the melted cube off of me. I felt her pull on my clit again as a small giggle escaped her, and then I looked down. I felt another piece of ice go inside of me and watched as Remy then grabbed the dildo. My pussy felt numb from the ice cu-bes, and as she placed a piece of ice on my clit and held it there, she glided the dildo inside of me. My wet pussy opened up easily for the toy. She pulled it out, only leaving the head inside, and then twisted it around, and then she rammed it back into me. "Oh, Remy. Fuck me bitch." She sucked on my clit as she fucked me with the black toy. It felt so good that I didn't want to cum just yet. "Yes, Robert. Oh, Robert, you feel so good."

I felt Remy stop. I looked down at Remy and could see the hurt in her eyes before she shoved the dick back inside of me. I acted as if I did nothing wrong and continued thrusting my hips. I could feel myself about to cum and wanted her to take my clit back in her mouth, but she was being stubborn now because of my slip up. I didn't say anything because I knew there was nothing I could say. I was dead wrong, so I just let the dick pound me until I felt myself cumming. I reached down and pulled on my own clit to intensify the orgasm. I could tell that she was just ready to get this over with. My cum gushed out all over the dildo and when I was done, she pulled it out and left the room. I knew I was wrong, but I couldn't help myself. I figured that I should probably give her some space and then tell her about this man who kept invading my space. If she cared anything about me, she would understand, but if not, fuck her. I left a little note for her to call me and to also apologize, and then walked out with one thing on my mind, a beautiful brown-skinned dread.

Chapter Twenty-One

When I walked into work the next morning, I was shocked to find Remy sitting at my desk waiting for me. She had never come to my job before, so this visit was a little unexpected. She started the conversation, "Who the fuck is Robert and why were you calling his name while I'm deep in your pussy?" Remy wasn't my woman. She was just a bitch I fucked, so I didn't know what gave her the right to question me. I knew she cared about me and I cared about her too, but she didn't own me.

I told her, "First of all, you have no right to question me about shit." I looked her in the eyes while talking, because I needed to make sure she knew I was serious. I then continued, "Robert is a nigga I can't seem to shake. I haven't even fucked him yet, well, unless you count my dreams." I continued by telling her how he made me feel. We talked about it for a few minutes and then made up. A true friendship never let anything come between it, especially a nigga.

"Where is that fine ass boss of yours?" she asked seductively while looking around.

I answered her in a curious manner. "He's out of town for a couple of days. Why you wanna know?"

She answered in typical Remy fashion, "Bitch, I'm trying to break his desk in."

I laughed and said, "I already did and girl, the dick is amazing." I then stood there thinking for a minute before grabbing her hand and saying, "Let's go."

As soon as we stepped in Jamal's office, Remy started getting naked. I locked the door behind me just in case. She picked up one of his ties that was hanging on the back of his chair and put it around her neck, letting it hang between her perky breasts. Wearing nothing but the tie, she swiveled the chair around one good time and then spread her legs over the armrests, one on each side, making her pussy open up. As I began by unbuttoning my blouse, I heard a key in the lock and before I could do anything, Jamal walked in. He stood in shock for a minute, looking at me, and then turned to look at Remy sprawled out in his chair. She was a nasty bitch and didn't care that she was violating his space with her bare ass. I was about to explain when Remy cut me off, "You came back just in time."

Jamal turned around, shut the door, and then locked it. I told Remy to get dressed, but Jamal chimed in, "Nah. You ain't gotta do nothing. Don't stop because of me." He paused and walked over beside his desk and continued, "Why don't you two lovely ladies show me what you were about to do."

Remy's freaky ass picked a highlighter up from off of his desk and began slapping her clit with it, and then rubbed it in between her pussy lips. "I was just gonna borrow this highlighter here to bring out some good points that needed a little touching on."

I looked down and saw Jamal's dick growing inside his pants. I walked over to him and began rubbing the back of his neck. I then went down and pressed my hand around his dick. It felt like it was ready to bust out of his zipper. I unzipped his pants and pulled it out through the slit in his boxers. I was going to work on his dick while Remy continued with her show. When I looked over at her, she had the highlighter inside of her pussy, going in and out. She was jacking her fat clit at the same time. The office was eerily quiet, and you could hear Remy's pussy juice squishing against the highlighter. I got down on my knees in front of Jamal and pulled him into my mouth, taking him all the way to the back of my throat. "Yes, Nicole. That shit feels good. Suck that dick harder."

I looked at Remy out the corner of my eyes, and it made me suck harder. I stopped only for a brief moment, so I could pull Jamal's pants completely off. I heard Remy moaning loud and knew that she was about to make herself cum. "Uh. Mmm. Uh."

After she came, I let Jamal fall from my mouth and finished getting undressed. I grabbed his hand and walked him over to the desk. I wanted Remy to experience some of this good dick Jamal carried around. "Get up and sit on top of the desk, Remy." When she did, she pulled her legs back up so her pussy would be open and ready. I grabbed Jamal's dick in my hand and guided him inside of her. "Ooh, yes." Remy held her head back while his dick went in and out of her. When I let go of Jamal's dick, he began to fuck her faster, and I heard Remy say, "Damn, nigga. This dick is good."

I reached behind Jamal between his legs and began tugging on his balls, my fingers pressing into them hard. Pulling on them like I was milking a cow. I then dropped his balls and stuck my finger inside my mouth, wetting it, and then I spread his ass cheeks and inserted it into his asshole. "Fuck." I felt his ass cheeks tighten a little, but he didn't make me pull my finger out. I fucked him while he fucked her, and then I reached around with my other hand and pinched his nipple. He rammed into Remy so hard, my finger fell out of him. He then pulled out and faced me and said, "Suck this shit, Nicole. Catch all of it too."

I put his dick in my mouth just in time to catch his seeds. His juices running down my throat quenched my thirst. I really wasn't in the dick sucking mood, so I put Remy on him. As she slurped on his dick and balls, I let him watch me suck on her pussy. I couldn't lie, every time I was with her, I had a blast. Damn, I was gonna miss this girl.

When we were done, Remy snatched up Jamal's tie and told him, "I'm keeping this for memories."

I knew that now since they were familiar with each other they would hook up again. I didn't know if I would be part of that little get together or not, but I damn sure wouldn't try to stop it. I was glad that she wasn't mad at me anymore, because this would be our last time hooking up until she got back from touring with The Money Boyz. I made her promise to call me before she left and to check in with me every couple of days. Two weeks would fly by, but little did I know, it would be more than two weeks before I would see her again.

Chapter Twenty-Two

Robert was cooking over tonight, and I was excited yet nervous. I was hoping that he would decide to stay all night again, because I wanted—no, I needed his arms around me holding me tight. Remy left this morning and I missed her already, so Robert's company was needed more than he knew. His presence would help me not worry so much about her. I heard my doorbell ring and when I opened it, there he stood looking like a professional gangster. He had on beige Dickies and a beige and black plaid button up. His beige and black Timbs seemed to make the outfit shine brighter. His dreads were braided up and as his bedroom eyes stared at me, I could already see myself pulling those braids down. When he licked those sexy ass lips, my pussy became instantly wet. I swear I came in my panties.

I looked down and saw that he was carrying an overnight bag and asked, "You look like you don't plan on leaving anytime soon."

He shrugged his broad shoulders and said, "I'll stay forever if you let me." His words caused my heart to speed up, and when he walked through the door and kissed me lightly upon my cheek, I thought I was going to have a heart attack. "I bought some groceries so I can cook you up some real food," he said as he held the bag up.

This nigga was capturing me more and more with each gesture. He was definitely getting this pussy tonight. It took me a minute, but I finally responded, "I never had a man cook for me before."

He came back with, "That's because you ain't never had a real man." I smiled as he continued, "But I got you, lil' mama." And then he proceeded to the kitchen.

I sat and watched as he prepared our food, barbeque chicken that fell off the bone, a taste of barbeque in every bite, white rice with some of the barbeque drizzle over the top, broccoli smothered in a creamy cheese sauce, and baked cornbread with bits of bacon and jalapeno peppers in it. This nigga threw down and I devoured every single bite. When we finished our meal, he asked, "Yo, you mind if I take a shower? I did a little work today and didn't have a chance to shower before I came over." Before I could answer, I imagined him covered in little droplets of water. Mmm. I would love to lick him dry. I broke from my trance by him calling my name. "Yo, Nicole. You alright?"

I was so embarrassed, and I knew the redness of my cheeks gave me away, but I responded anyway, "Uh, um, yeah. Take as long as you need."

He then went into the bathroom and left me standing there, wet pussy and all. He left the bathroom door open and to me, that was an invitation to look, so I took advantage of it. I could see his manly form through the clear shower curtain, and as if he felt me watching him, he turned his head to me.

I was stuck and couldn't pull myself away, although I had been caught red handed. Suddenly, he opened the shower curtain, causing me to jump. The water was hot and caused steam to escape from the open space. Suds rested on his body, causing me to feel a bit jealous. I tried my hardest not to venture lower, but my eyes betrayed me. His dick was perfectly formed in length and width, and I wanted to touch it so bad. He smiled, and them damn butterflies began fluttering in the pit of my stomach again. He motioned for me to come to him and said, "Don't just stand there. I think there's room for one more."

I was not going to make him ask me twice. I took off my clothes and walked to him, and as he grabbed my hand to help me step inside, my clit pulsed. He immediately pulled me to him, kissing me with a passion that couldn't be explained. My breathing sped up, my clit painfully throbbed, and my nipples were about to burst with pleasure. He pulled away and grabbed his dick, gently jacking it back and forth. I inhaled his scent as he spoke to me. "I've been waiting for you my whole life."

His words feel so real yet so unheard of, and I didn't know how to respond, so I didn't. Instead, I pulled him down to me, back into a passionate kiss. His luscious lips demanded my mouth to submit. I was lost and didn't know what to do. I was anticipating his next move so that I could follow his lead. He pulled from me again and then reached his big strong hand between my thighs. He rubbed lightly across my clit and then told me, "Let's go to the bedroom. This ain't where I want our first time to be."

He was so unbelievably romantic, and I didn't know how to respond. I'd never had someone treat me like this, but I liked this feeling. I looked up at him and then turned to step out of the shower. He was close behind me, following my steps.

When I got to the bed, I turned to face him. I could feel his breathing in my face as he looked down at me from his tall frame. He placed his hands on my shoulders and then ran them the length of my arms. We looked in each other's eyes, and it was so quiet I swore I could hear my heartbeat. He told me, "Lie down, Nicole."

And I did, like an obedient wife would do for her husband. He took my legs and bent them at the knees, pushing them up to my chest in the softest manner I had ever felt. He then dropped down to his knees, and before his mouth even touched me, I came. This had never happened before, but I couldn't seem to control my body whenever I was in his presence. His touch was strong and demanding, and I'd longed for him forever. He said nothing as his tongue found my clit. As he flicked it over my little pearl, I swore I could see stars shining above me. He then sucked it softly into his mouth, and a single tear dropped from my eyes, not because it hurt, but because I had never felt something so damn good in my life. "Yes, Robert. Oh, baby, it feels so good." As my words betrayed me and fell from my lips, I felt a finger slide inside of me. He found my G-spot instantly, as if he had traveled there before, and once again, "I'm cumming."

He got up and sat on the bed beside me at first, and then leaned back against the headboard. I got up and faced him and crawled over to him and straddled his lap. I put my arms around his neck, and as I brought my mouth to his, I lifted up and let his dick find its home. Although he's not, it felt as if he was the first man to ever embrace my essence. He filled me up completely, leaving no room for anyone else behind him. I rode him slowly as he gripped my ass cheeks with his big, strong hands. "Damn, Nicole. You were well worth the wait," he said to me, giving me an extra boost of confidence.

I sped up and rode him hard, slamming down onto him. "Mmm, Robert. You feel so good inside of me." I could feel the pulse of his dick inside and I knew he was about to cum. I couldn't seem to come off of him as I continued to ride. I had never let a man cum inside of me, but I didn't want to let him go. I wanted him to fill me with all he had inside of him. I didn't want to lose one single drop, because I was afraid he would share it with another, and I wanted it all just for me. "Uh. Oh god, ooh," I screamed out to him.

"I'm cumming, Nicole. I'm about to cum all in this pussy." I didn't stop as his seeds filled my insides. I kept riding because I wanted this to be the best orgasm of his life. At that moment, I didn't care about babies or diseases. I just knew I couldn't lose a single drop. I knew better, but all I cared about right now was this nigga under me and inside of me. When he was completely drained, I finally came off of him. We lay down in the bed and he was behind me, holding me, and I didn't know where the words came from, but I said to him, "Can we stay like this forever?"

Chapter Twenty-Three

After that night, Robert and I became inseparable. Everything about him was different than any other man I'd ever encountered. He was perfect, and as much as I hated to say it, I felt myself falling in love with him. I vowed all my life to never fall in love, but with Robert, I couldn't stop myself. My mama was heartbroken by my daddy, and to experience the pain she went through made me never want to love a man. I didn't want to bear the type of agony she suffered. She was never the same again, and I vowed that it would never happen to me, but I just couldn't stop my feelings.

I had gotten a call from Remy telling me that the tour was being extended for two more weeks but she was good. I missed Remy like crazy, but Robert kept me from being lonely. I'd had a long day at work and couldn't wait to get home. When I walked in the front door, I heard the shower going and went to find my man. Robert said the shower always took his mind to another place. I peeked through one door but didn't say anything. I wanted to surprise him when he came out, so I stripped down and then put on a hot pink teddy and lay down on the bed to wait for him. He came out of the bathroom naked, running a towel over his dreads, and as soon as I saw his wet, sexy body I spread my legs and began playing with my clit. I looked him in the eyes and smiled, saying, "Momma's home."

He dropped the towel from his hands and walked over to the bed and crawled on it as if he was the king of the lions. He was so fucking sexy as he pushed my legs apart even wider and said, "Daddy's been waiting on this pussy all day."

He sucked my clit into his mouth so hard it hurt, and I flinched a little from the pain. He then moved his tongue down to my hole and pushed it inside. "Oh, baby, yes. Yes." As his tongue went in and out of me like a dick, his thumb pressed hard on my clit, causing an instant rush. "Baby, I'm cumming. Yes, baby. Yes," I screamed as my juice squirted out onto his tongue. He didn't let up until I was completely drained. "Turn over and let me show daddy what's real."

I was so ready for his dick to be in my mouth, and as soon as he turned over, I wasted no time devouring his prized piece. I went as deep as I could, and as the head brushed against my tonsils, I gagged a little but refused to stop. He put his hands on the back of my head and gently pushed as I felt his vein pulsing. I came off of him because I wanted him inside of me. "Come on, baby. Let me fuck you from the back," he told me as I assumed the position.

I flinched as he entered me, and as always, it felt like my first time. I took in all of him as he went in and out, over and over. I could feel my heart beating faster, and I called his name, "Robert. Yes, baby."

I reached my hand down between my legs and began to play with my clit as he beat my pussy up. I could hear him grunting and moaning behind me, "Mmm, shit. Yeah." He was slamming into me now and then stopped moving as he emptied his seeds into me once again. I didn't complain because that's where they belonged. He could plant them in my garden always.

The next day, we decided that we would go visit a new upscale club that had just opened. We hadn't been out in a couple of weeks, so we needed the escape. Remy had been calling every day and she seemed to be doing really well. She said that she had fallen for one of the rappers and was going to start working on getting herself together. I was so happy for her and couldn't wait until she got home. I told her about the feelings I had for Robert, and it made her happy that I had found someone so good. After we hung up, I decided I should start getting ready for the night.

When we made it to the club, it was packed. I was worried about finding a parking spot, but Robert had status and was able to park around back with club personnel. He also took us in through the back door and before we made it all the way in, he stopped and turned to me, kissing me like he had never done it before, and like it would be his last kiss. The club was so packed there was barely any walking room. We got a table in VIP and he ordered us drinks. "Give Me You" by Mary J. came over the speakers, so Robert grabbed my hand and led me to the dance floor. His arms around my waist fit perfectly, and I knew I wanted them there forever. He bent his head to my ear and whispered, "I'm in love with you, Nicole."

I stiffened as a tear fell from my eye. No man other than my father had ever told me they loved me. I pulled from him and looked up into his eyes and said, "I'm in love with you, Robert," and then we kissed until the song ended. We stayed about another hour and then left. Robert had drank a little more than me, so I opted to drive us home. It was dark and my head was light, so I drove a little faster than usual. We only had six more blocks to go because we decided to go to Robert's condo instead of mine, which was a little farther away. My pussy was wet, and I couldn't wait until his dick got inside of me.

I turned on the road that his condo was located on and out of nowhere, a truck came into view. I swerved to avoid it and saw a man on a bike. I then swerved again to avoid him too, but it was too late. The impact knocked me out for a few minutes and when I woke, I looked beside me. "Robert. Oh my god, Robert."

His bloody face brought tears to my eyes and sudden pains to my heart. Robert wasn't moving, and I couldn't move to reach him. I heard the sirens in the background and prayed for them to hurry up to save him, because I couldn't imagine a life without him now. Could I have really hit that bike that hard to do this much damage? Then I remembered the pole and the impact. Was I going that fast? I was scared to death, so as the sirens came into view, I breathed a sigh of relief and waited...

***

Nine months later

It was hard walking in shackles, but it was required to be transported. My ankles were killing me, and I knew they had to be raw from the shackles rubbing against them. Them crackers gave me fifteen years for two DUI manslaughters. I would do half of that if I showed good behavior during my stay. The man on the bike didn't make it, and I lost Robert. I had also lost the child that Robert and I made out of love, a child I didn't know I was carrying. This prison would now be my home until they let me go. I now knew what a broken heart felt like, and it was the worst thing I'd ever felt. I knew

I had to make the best of a bad situation, so I did as I was told. Being processed in was a motherfucker, and I was glad when it was over. I had lost everything that had meant anything to me. Remy was about to get married and have a baby of her own. Robert was in the ground, and I was all by myself and no longer cared about life. I got put in my own cell for the first few days because they thought I was going to harm myself, but no matter what, I loved me.

The guard came a few days later and told me to pack my things so I could go to general population. I was ready fast because being alone gave me too much time to think, and thinking made me hurt inside even more. I was taken to GP and when I saw my new bunkie, it made me tingle a little. This bitch looked like a straight nigga and reminded me a little of Robert. Her name was Treyanna, but she went by Trey for short. She told me that her girlfriend lived in the cell next to us and not to mind her when she trips. Which apparently she did a lot.

I had never been around so many bitches before in my life, and I had already seen a few that I couldn't wait to spread these pussy lips for. I didn't give a fuck anymore and was going to do what I wanted. I saw a couple of guards I was going to let run up in this too. There was no way I was going to stay here all these years and not get some dick. Hell no.

Trey had dreads, and every time I looked at them, I thought of Robert's dreads clenched between my fingers as he made sweet love to me. Robert was the first man I had ever felt anything for, and now he and the child we would have shared were gone. I was going back to who I was before I met him, and I didn't give a fuck who I hurt in the process.

Trey turned out to be a pretty cool bunkie, and we got along great. Her girlfriend didn't like me, so because of that, I was going to make it my business to fuck Trey as often as I could. I decided that tonight, I was going to make my move. She had the top bunk, and I was going to make enough noise to wake her and cause her to look down at me. When the cell doors locked and the cell lights went out, I waited only a few minutes and started my performance. I pulled my panties to the side and pulled on my clit while pressing it between my fingers. I then went a little lower and slid a finger inside of my wet pussy. The sound of my juices echoed in the silent room. I pulled my finger out and went back to my clit, jacking it fast and moaning loud enough to be heard, "Mmm, mmm, yes." I peeked out of one of my eyes and saw Trey leaning over from her top bunk. I didn't even stop what I was doing as I opened both eyes and looked at her while asking, "Did I wake you?"

She then disappeared from my view and jumped down from her bunk and just stood there. I turned my head to her and said between breaths, "I'm having a little trouble here. Wanna help?"

She just stood there staring and weighing her options before getting on the bunk with me. I spread my legs wide, but Trey closed them and then reached up, pulling my panties completely off before spreading them again. She first pushed a finger into my asshole and went in and out a few times before pushing her thumb into my pussy. It had been a while since I had been penetrated, so my pussy was good and tight. I rotated my hips to the rhythm of her fingers as I heard her ask, "Is this where you need help at?"

Trey finally pulled her fingers out of me, and I could see my wetness embracing them under the dim cell light. She bent her head down between my thighs and pulled on my clit with her lips. When she began sucking on it, I caught chills all over my body. I could understand why her girlfriend tripped now. This bitch could suck some pussy real good. I then remembered that her girl lived right next door to us, so my moaning got louder. "Yes, oh yes. Right there. Suck this pussy good. Yes." I knew she could hear me, but I didn't give a fuck about her. I wanted her to hear what her nigga was doing to me after lights out. What was she going to do? Straighten me? She better check her bitch first.

At that moment, I felt someone watching me and opened my eyes. I saw the guard standing at the door staring into our cell, but I didn't say anything to Trey. Instead, I lifted up my shirt and began twisting my nipples between my fingers. I bet his dick was hard as fuck and imagined it deep in my pussy. I wanted him to enjoy his little show, so I pushed my breast up and started flicking my tongue over my nipple, and then sucked it into my mouth. That mother-fucker had to reach up and wipe the sweat off of his forehead. I mouthed to him. "Come fuck me." He smiled as I fucked Trey's mouth. I could feel the orgasm building up inside of me and told Trey, "Oh, shit. Trey, I'm cumming."

She sucked even harder as my pussy juice squirted out of me. She let my clit go and licked my entire pussy clean with the same mouth she would be kissing her bitch with tomorrow. The thought made me giggle inside. The guard finally walked away, probably to go hide out somewhere and jack his dick. I knew he wished that he was between these thighs, and who knows, maybe one day I could make his wish come true.

Chapter Twenty-Four

The next day, Mr. Turner, the guard that was peeking through my cell window the night before, came on duty and was assigned to my dorm. He shouted out in the dorm that he needed a volunteer. I knew this would be my opportunity to get some dick, so I happily raised my hand. He had me walking around the grounds of the prison picking up trash. The compound was pretty big, and I was curious as to when he would make his move. I was ready for some dick but didn't want to be the first one to make a move, so I chilled. We ended up behind one of the old buildings that was no longer lived in, and that was when he approached the subject. "I saw you and your bunkie last night engaging in a sex act." He paused and looked at me then continued in an authoritative tone, "That's a rule violation."

I raised an eyebrow and asked, "What's your point?"

He hesitated before speaking again, as if he needed to get the right words together. "I really don't want to write you up, so I was thinking about some extra duty instead."

I shrugged my shoulders at his comment and asked, "What does my extra duty consist of, sir?"

"Well, inmate, I'll let you decide what you want to do."

I stepped closer to him and began to rub his hardening dick through his pants and said, "I'm pretty good on my knees, Mr. Turner, so maybe I could perform a job while on them."

I chuckled at the comment I made and then unzipped his pants. He didn't try to stop me as I pulled his dick out through the slit in his boxers, and although it wasn't very thick, the length made up for it. I looked up into his eyes before dropping to my knees. I inhaled his manly scent as I licked around the head and then up and down his shaft. The clean smell of him turned me on even more.

I pulled just the head of him into my mouth and sucked lightly as my tongue brushed against his pre-cum. I could hear a moan escaping his lips. "Mmm, hmm." I began pushing the rest of him into my mouth, but he was too long for me to go all the way. His dick disappeared and then reappeared. He grabbed the back of my head and tried pushing all the way into me, but I gagged. His dick was just too long. I had to push him back some because my eyes were beginning to water from gagging. I sucked harder and faster until he told me he was about to cum. "I'm cumming. Catch that shit and swallow." I couldn't wait to swallow his salty cum down my throat.

Mr. Turner sure knew how to work his dick, and I couldn't wait until he worked it inside my pussy. I knew that day would come soon enough. As the thoughts of fucking him filled my head, his cum shot out and filled my mouth, filling me with protein. I didn't let him pull out until I swallowed every drop. It was time to head back to the dorm because they would be calling count soon. When I walked into the housing unit, I could hear Trey and her bitch arguing. I walked past them smiling and headed for our cell to prepare myself just in case the bitch wanted to try me. I sat down on the toilet to take a piss and sure enough, here came Trey's bitch. She didn't even let me get off the toilet before she was bending down all in my face, going off about hearing me moaning through the walls. I didn't know what Trey told her, but I had my own story, "Bitch, I don't know what you think happened nor do I give a fuck, but if my ass wants to play in my pussy, I know you gon' let me."

She suddenly stopped selling out and just stared at me. Then she looked at Trey and stormed out of the cell. I lied to her because I wasn't about to fuck myself out of some more good head. I refused to ruin what I had going on, and since it seemed that her girlfriend was satisfied with my response, I figured that I was good. I heard Trey after she walked out of the cell behind her and said, "I told you."

Oh yeah, this nigga was going to fuck me good tonight for this one. I finally finished pissing and got up and washed my hands. I then decided to lie down for a little while and maybe even take a nap. Before I could close my eyes good, they had called count and Trey walked back in the cell. She thanked me for lying and said she owed me one. I told her that she could pay me back tonight after lights out. This time, I wasn't gonna lie about it.

After lights out, I watched as Trey took a toothbrush holder and began wrapping it with sanitary pads. After the pads were snugly around it, she covered it with a latex glove. She slid it over the wrapped holder like it was a condom being put on a dick. When she was completely done, it looked like a dick, a nice thick one at that. That shit was crazy to me, and I would never forget it. Just watching her form it had me soaking wet.

Trey was sexy as fuck, and she looked just like a nigga. I loved her thuggish ways and couldn't understand why she was with the bitch next door. I was determined to fuck Trey every day, whether she had a bitch or not. She got out a bra next and attached the tooth-brush holder to it before wrapping it around her hips. She made sure it was extra secure by wrapping a rubber band around the base. She looked like a man with a real dick, and I couldn't wait to feel her inside of me.

I wanted it from the back, so I turned around and got on all fours. She bent down and ran her wet tongue from my ass crack to my clit. Just enough for her spit to coat me and just long enough to tease me. Trey definitely knew how to use her tongue, no wonder I couldn't get enough of her. I bet she could use the strap just as good. She inserted a finger inside of me and guided it in and out. She then pulled it out and sucked all of my juice off of it. When I felt the tip of the strap-on at the entrance of my pussy, I became more excited. She pushed it into me slowly and gently, as if she would break me, but my pussy wasn't fragile. I wanted her to beat it up. When it was all the way in, she stopped and spread my ass cheeks. I felt it as her thumb went into my asshole. "Oh, god. Fuck me, Trey." She pulled her thumb in and out a few times before she started working the strap-on again. It was as if she was teasing me, but I didn't feel like being teased. I wanted to be fucked. She kept building me up just to bring me down. I turned my head back and told her angrily, "Bitch, you gonna fuck this pussy or not?"

She then pulled her thumb out of me, grabbed my ass cheeks really tight, and rammed the built-up strap-on into me. She hit the walls of my pussy like a pro, and I had to tell her, "That's right, Trey, fuck this pussy like a real nigga. Yes." I reached my hand down and played with my clit as she tore my pussy up. I felt myself about to cum and braced myself. "I'm cumming, Trey. Please don't stop now. I'm cumming." Our sweat covered bodies were sticking together as her thighs met the back of mine and then, there was a knock at the wall.

I guess her girlfriend could hear our little session. As a matter of fact, I knew she did because I made it my business to ensure that she did. Her little knock on the wall stopped nothing. I pushed back on Trey as she met my thrust. When she came, her body shook like thunder and mad goose bumps appeared on my skin. She pulled the cum-soaked homemade dildo out of me, then leaned back and tried to catch her breath. There was no way I was going to let her bitch stop me from getting fucked. This shit was too good to leave alone. Trey finally got up off of my bed and dismantled the dildo. She flushed everything down the stainless steel toilet except the tooth-brush holder. I was amazed at the power the holder had and couldn't wait to experience it again. We were exhausted and decided to get some rest. We knew that tomorrow was going to bring a lot of drama, and we needed to be ready.

Chapter Twenty-Five

As soon as the cell doors opened the next morning, Trey's girlfriend ran in swinging. I swerved and it caused her to punch the wall instead. "Ow, shit."

I didn't know why the bitch was mad at me. I didn't owe her a damn thing. She swung again, and this time she made her target and busted me in the mouth. "You bitch," I said as I punched her dead in the eye, and then I kept pounding my fists into her face until I felt the spray hitting me.

My eyes were on fire along with my face and arms. I knew they didn't think I was gonna let that bitch put her hands on me and not do anything about it. Fuck that. I'm gonna always defend myself and couldn't care less about the consequences.

The guards separated us and cuffed us up and walked us to confinement. There's no way that Trey gave a shit about her because while I was beating her ass, she did nothing to help her. We stopped by medical on the way to confinement so the nurse could check us out. My lip was swollen and hurt like a motherfucker, but I tried not to show any weakness or pain. When we made it to confinement, they put us in a cold water shower to wash the pepper spray up off of us. As soon as the old water hit my nipples, they stood at attention. I noticed the female guard watching me, so I decided to give her a show. I turned my back to the water and faced her, twisting my nipple between my fingers. I didn't even know if she got down like that, but she didn't take her eyes off of me.

I used that to my advantage and placed one leg up on the shower wall and spread my pussy lips. My clit poked out, as if peeking at her. I pulled the hood back and licked my finger before placing it on top of my clit. I maintained eye contact with her as I slowly massaged my swollen bud. She shook her head and smiled while standing there. I knew she wasn't trying to draw attention to me, because she wanted to see the whole show. I started jerking my clit really fast and silently mouthed the words, "I'm cumming," so that no one could hear me, and then squirted all down my thighs. The water quickly erased the misdeed that I had just engaged in.

I was taken to a single cell where they said I would be housed until the matter was investigated. I lay down because there wasn't shit else to do, and Robert suddenly entered my mind as my eyes slowly closed. He was there already naked, walking to me. His dick moving side to side as if keeping in tune with his steps. I could see his balls peeking out, as if trying to find a way to escape. I was lying on my stomach watching him as he got closer, and then I sat up to face him. His dick was sticking out like a ten millimeter pointed in my face, waiting for the trigger to be pulled.

I didn't reach out and grab it with my hand. No, I stuck my tongue out and lifted it with all the strength I could find. I let my tongue pull the weight of it into my mouth, and then I used one hand to cup his dangling gems. I used my other hand to grab his shaft as I sucked only the head. I let it go and lined my lips with his pre-cum and then sucked it back into my mouth. I looked up and met his gaze as I pulled it out of mouth once again, guiding my tongue along the edges of the head, and then stuck the point of my tongue over the little hole and licked it. His pre-cum was only an appetizer for me. I was shooting for the whole meal, though, so I guided him back into my mouth. This time, taking all of him in.

"Inmate Waters. Inmate Waters." I could vaguely hear my name being called and realized that a guard was at my door. "Inmate Waters. The warden wants you in his office." I was pissed because my dreams were the only time I had with Robert, and I didn't like that time being disturbed. I was slowly trying to forget him and move on because I needed to. I needed to be able to live my life, and with him constantly invading my dreams, it was making it so hard to do.

I got dressed and turned around to be cuffed up and was then escorted to the warden's office. I was actually surprised when I walked in and saw him. I expected an old man with scraggly hair and maybe even a beard. This dude was actually kind of sexy for a white man. I could see the outline of his wife beater through his dress shirt. The officer directed me to stand in front of the warden's desk and not to speak unless asked. He stood me there with the cuffs still on my wrists and attempted to walk out. The warden stopped him and told him to take the restraints off of me before he left, and he did as he said. He told him that he would radio him when he was done questioning me about the incident that happened.

After the guard left, the warden went over to the door and locked it. He turned back to me and walked up so close to me I could smell the mint on his breath. He started running a finger down my cheek, telling me that he could make the disciplinary report disappear. This white boy actually had chills going up my spine with just the little touch of his finger. I knew that I wasn't leaving his office today until I fucked him.

I reached over and started unbuttoning his shirt, revealing the wife beater. His small nipples poked out from the thin fabric. I sucked one of them into my mouth, wetting the wife beater and leaving a small wet spot. I then undid his belt and let the trousers he had on drop to the floor below and crumple at his feet. He stepped all the way out of them and then ordered me to undress. His dick was hard and pushing through the peephole of his boxers, a small pink eye at the tip looking at me with pre-cum oozing out. I had sucked a lot of dick, but none so small and so pink. I was pissed and wondered what I was supposed to do with something this little. How could a man this sexy have such a small dick? I didn't want to embarrass him, and I wanted out of confinement with no paperwork. So, I was going to put on a show and make him feel really good. I grabbed it with my hand and it literally disappeared in my grasp. I wanted to laugh but maintained my composure. I sucked the whole thing into my mouth at once. I was afraid to suck it too hard, fearing I would suck it off and it would fall down my throat. I was hoping this white boy would cum quick so I could get this over with.

When he was all the way hard, he forcibly turned me around and pressed his body into mine before shoving his dick up my ass. I didn't even flinch because his little man felt like a finger inside of me. About two minutes later, he was cumming all over my ass cheeks, leaving a stench that made me want to vomit. He then walked over to his desk and pulled out some Handi Wipes and told me to clean myself up. I wondered how many other inmates he had done this to as I cleaned his liquid off of me.

He called over the radio for the guard to come back and get me, and I was so glad when he got there and took me back to my cell. I was released from confinement the next day, and Trey's girlfriend was shipped off the compound. I was put right back in the cell with Trey, which made me very happy. Getting fucked by the warden really paid off, and I would continue to use it to my advantage.

Trey acted like she was upset about her girlfriend leaving, but not enough to ignore me. We ended up taking a shower together that night and when the cell door closed, it was business as usual. This time, I wanted to taste Trey. She said she got off by making someone else feel good, but I loved eating pussy and begged her to let me do it. Her clit was really small and as soon as I sucked it into my mouth, Trey jumped at my touch. I went to slide a finger in her and she stopped me, telling me that her pussy had never been penetrated, and that made me want to do it even more.

She allowed me to use one finger only, and when I stuck it inside her, it was really tight. I knew she had told me the truth right then. It only took a couple of minutes for her to get wet enough for me to glide my finger in and out with ease. I licked, sucked, and fucked Trey like she had never been done before. I wanted to turn her all the way out, but there would be time for that. I could tell that Trey was really feeling me, but after Robert, there was never going to be anyone else I could be serious with.

The next day, I had a legal call from an attorney who wanted to get me back in court. He said that a female named Remiah Williams had hired him. My heart skipped a beat, because I thought Remy had forgotten about me. I went back to the cell and shared my news with Trey. I had already told her all about Remy, so she knew who I was talking about. I told her if I got out, I would keep it real with her, and then when she got out, she could join me and Remy for a little rendezvous.

Chapter Twenty-Six

I was put on the docket the next day to get a job, and they ended up placing me in a canteen store. I guess because of my high TABE scores. I thought about Jamal and wondered if he had found someone else to cheat on Terry with, and if he was sharing her. I had heard that he got a temp to take my place until I got out of here. I liked the fact that he was hoping I'd come back to work for him. I bet he couldn't find someone to suck and fuck him like me, though.

I showed up the next morning and was inventoried into the store and given my key. I got the store together to shop the other inmates, and I must say, I did a damn good job. At the end of the day, after shutting down, I began to daydream about what it would be like to fuck not one but two officers in my store. A sudden knock broke my thoughts and brought me back to the present. It was a fine ass officer coming to count me in my store. Because of my daydream, I had lost track of the time and got stuck. He saw that my cheeks were flushed and asked if I was okay. I told him that I had been daydreaming about getting some dick in my store, wondering what it would be like.

He said, "Give me a minute to call in count and I'll show you what it's like." He then came in, locking the door behind him. "I've been thinking about you ever since you first got here," he said to me while smiling.

I responded seductively, "Why don't you tell me what you thought."

It looked as if he got nervous when he said, "I thought about putting you up on that counter and tasting that pussy."

I smiled and walked up to him, grabbing him by the hand, and said, "That sounds good. Why don't I give you a tester." We walked to the back of the store and he pulled me into a kiss. He pulled my bottom lip into his mouth and then started caressing my breast. He was being very dominant, and I could feel it all the way down to my thighs. My panties were soaked from the wetness he had caused.

He reached and pulled my pants and panties down and then told me to step out of them. "Yes, Officer," I responded innocently.

He lifted me in his arms, and as he applied little kisses to my cheek and neck, he sat me on the counter and told me, "Lay back and enjoy."

He lifted up my shirt and bra, exposing my hardened nipples, and began pinching on them really hard. It felt so good as he leaned over and pulled one into his mouth, wetting it and then blowing on it, giving it a cool sensation. He flicked his tongue over it and then sucked it until I was almost ready to cum. As he went from nipple to nipple, he took two fingers and pushed them into me. "Oh my god, Officer. This feels so good."

He responded, "Shut up and just enjoy it." His fingers were fucking me nice and slow, hitting my walls. He was moving them in a circular motion as he added another one to the party. As his fingers invaded me, he took his thumb and pressed hard on my clit. I was so wet that I could feel my juices draining down to my asshole, wetting it too. He pulled on my clit now with his other hand, and I tightened my muscles and told him, "Shit. I'm about to cum."

He pulled his fingers out of me and put them to my mouth. "Suck the cum off of them." He just didn't know, I loved tasting my own pussy, and I sucked and licked them dry. My cum was a treat for me. He pulled me closer to the edge of the counter and dropped his head between my legs and buried it in my pussy. He was sucking my clit really hard, and I knew if he kept it up, I was going to cum even harder. I didn't even have time to tell him before my cum squirted out all over his chin. He kept sucking my clit and then inserted his thumb in my pussy and his pointer finger in my ass, pulling them in and out until my massive orgasm was over.

He got up, licked his lips, and said, "Now keep this our little secret."

I agreed and said, "Your turn."

He undid his pants and pulled them down as I got on my knees in front of him. He began stroking his dick and then spanked my lips with it. I pulled him into my mouth as he stated, " I don't want to cum too quick, so take your time." He pulled me up off the floor by a handful of my hair and then bent me over the counter. He spread my ass cheeks apart and rammed his long, hard dick into me, causing me to grunt, "Uh. Shit," and then he slid it in and out real slow. I told him, "Nigga, stop teasing me." He then sped up and slammed his massive package into me. "Yes. That's what I'm talking about."

He pumped into my pussy so hard that his balls were winging and slamming into my clit, giving it extra pleasure. All you could hear was skin against skin slapping together. I was throwing it back to him and meeting each thrust. "Mmm, yes. Fuck me, nigga."

He told me to be quieter because he didn't want anyone to hear us. I didn't know how he expected me to be quiet when the dick he was delivering was so damn good. He reached his hand up and put it over my mouth, trying to muffle the sounds. I felt myself cumming as my cream covered his beautiful black rod. He felt my pussy muscles contracting against him and pulled out, shooting his seeds all over my ass cheeks.

We wet some paper towels and cleaned ourselves up as he heard his name being called over the radio. He smiled at me and said, "Counts clear, until next time," and then he left out, as if nothing ever happened. I went back to the dorm a few minutes later, carrying my secret with me. I made dinner that night for me and Trey and then went and took a shower before lying down. Trey wanted to fuck, but I needed to catch up on some rest. She was disappointed, but I told her that I would make it up to her, and she knew I would.

While sleeping, I went into a dream about the sex I'd had with the officer. I definitely wanted to fuck him again. Maybe even in the shower with one of his buddies. No sooner than I started my dream about the two officers, I woke up. I was told that I needed to report to my store. I couldn't figure out why because I was supposed to be closed today, but I forgot it was a holiday and I would have to shop the inmates. I took a shower and got dressed and went to the store. At the end of the day, I was getting ready to leave and the officer I had fucked the day before showed up with another sexy, caramel-colored officer. He had to have been new to the compound, because I hadn't seen him before. He told me that when they came to the dorm later, for me to volunteer picking up supplies. I said okay and then locked up so I could go back to the dorm.

No sooner than I got out of the shower, I heard them ask for a volunteer to go get supplies. I knew that this would be my chance to fuck the sexy caramel brother, and I didn't pass up on many opportunities. I volunteered and then grabbed the cart so I could walk with them to the supply room. As I was loading the cart, the caramel brother looked at me and licked his lips and told me that he thought I was fine. He turned to his co-worker and asked, "Yo, dawg, you think we got enough time to spare so I can get my dick sucked?"

The officer told him in response, "Hell yeah. This shit's too damn good not to be shared." He paused, then continued, "Man, I hit that shit yesterday, and it's well worth it." He said it like I wasn't even sitting there, and if I would have had a low self-esteem, I would have taken offense.

The caramel brother summoned me over to the other side of the property room where there was a row of concrete benches. He told me, "Get on your knees and show me what you working with."

I was nervous and excited at the same time, but I loved the way a dick felt in my mouth. While I sucked on Mr. Caramel's dick, the other officer that I had fucked the day before just stood back and watched. My saliva coated Mr. Caramel's dick and was causing it to shimmer in the dim lighting. I looked out the corner of my eyes and saw the other officer approaching. He came over to the bench and sat beside his friend and said to me, "Yeah, Waters. Suck his dick good like you did mine." He started rubbing on his own dick through his BDUs and said, "You be a good girl, I might just give you a repeat of yesterday."

As I was holding Mr. Caramel's dick in my mouth, I started pulling his pants further down. I then spread his legs a little further and cupped his balls in my hand. I was kneading them as if they were dough and I was making biscuits. I dropped his dick out of my mouth and went down to his balls, licking them as if they were apples hanging from a tree. Pre-cum was forming on his dick, so I went up and licked the slimy substance off. I continued jacking the shaft of his dick and sucked on the head like a lollipop at the same time. I slurped and smacked inch by inch, until his entire length had disappeared. I didn't even gag as it brushed against my tonsils. I was enjoying this just as much as he was. He ran his fingers through my hair and then gripped it in his fist. I kept him buried in my mouth as my hands pulled on his balls.

I finally let him come out of my mouth halfway but continued sucking him nice and slow. I ran my teeth gently over the head of his dick, and he shuddered, as if I gave him chills. I could feel the vein pulsing and let his dick go and sucked one of his balls into my mouth. "Shit, girl. I'm gonna fucking cum."

I giggled and dropped his balls from my mouth, and then started sucking on his dick again as I jacked it with my hand at the same time. I sucked on him with no mercy, and swear I could feel his toes curl up in his work boots. His partner wasn't saying anything as he sat back and waited his turn. I sucked his dick all the way to the base and came all the way off of it, making a popping sound with my mouth. All of a sudden, his cum started shooting out, and I took him all the way back in as his seeds flowed down my throat with ease. I didn't waste a single drop. He told the other officer that he wanted to hit the pussy, too, one day. When he was done cumming, I let him fall out of my mouth and smiled, knowing there wasn't another bitch alive who would suck his dick like me.

The officer I had fucked the day before wanted his turn now, and I said, "Okay, but I think we should do something a little different."

He said in response, "Oh, yeah? Well, why don't you show me what it is."

I pulled off my pants and then my panties, and told him to stand in front of me. I undid his pants and pulled his hardened dick out of them. I kneeled in front of him, and before I could get him in my mouth, Mr. Caramel came behind me and pulled my hair back so he could get a good view. I turned my head and asked, "What you gonna do with this pussy?"

I then sucked the dick into my mouth in a slow, sensual manner. I only did it for a few seconds and then stopped. I told Mr. Caramel to sit on the bench, and I turned my ass to face him. However, instead of going into my pussy like I thought he would, he stuck it in my ass. It hurt a little because it had been a while since something had been up there. I flinched when he entered. His partner got back in front of me and bent his knees, squatting halfway down. He reached out and started playing with my clit, and it excited me, making me ride the dick inside of me harder. "You a freaky ass bitch," the officer in front of me said, and it only motivated me even more.

Mr. Caramel said he'd never fucked anyone in the ass before, but he liked it. The officer in front of me stuck two fingers into my pussy, and the feelings I was having were so intense, I swear I could feel it in my gut. A burning sensation was coursing through my body, and I started riding Mr. Caramel even faster. The officer in front of me inserted a third finger into me, and it took me over the edge. I started moaning and told them, "Mmm, hmmm, I'm cumming. Yes, I'm cumming." Mr. Caramel and I ended up cumming together, and it felt so good.

The officer in front of me pulled his fingers out of me and put them in his mouth. "Damn, you taste good."

I laughed and told him, "I know." I climbed up off the dick and went to get some tissue to clean myself off with, and turned around to tell them that we would do this again. We all cleaned up and left out of the property room to take the supplies back to the dorm. I wondered if anyone noticed how long we were gone, but the thought quickly left my mind because I really didn't give a fuck. When we got back to the dorm, we went our separate ways.

As I was making myself some dinner, I heard the officer call me to his station. When I got there, he told me that I needed to get some rest because once everyone went to sleep, I would be covering shower detail. I just shook my head, smiled, and walked away. I ate and went to my cell to get some much-needed rest like I was told to do. As soon as I closed my eyes, I went straight into a dream. It began with Remy and me. We were in a bedroom that I didn't recognize, and she was behind me, holding me close to her. She was holding me really tight, as if she would lose me if she loosened up. I sure missed her and couldn't wait to see her again.

My dream then shifted to Jamal and Terry, and our little rendezvous came into view. Jamal knew he had some good dick. I couldn't wait until it was inside of me again. I suddenly woke up to a wet pussy and a burning desire to cum. My cell door was un-locked, so I left the cell and went to use the dormitory bathroom instead of my own. When I sat on the toilet and pissed, I wiped my-self and then started playing with my clit. I leaned back and stretched out my legs while pinching and pulling on my little pearl. I was thinking of all my past sexual partners and then inserted two fingers into my wet hole. It was tight, although I had just gotten fingered earlier.

I began finger fucking myself slowly as my wetness coated my small fingers. It felt so good, and I took my other hand and rolled my clit between my thumb and pointer finger. I moved my hips to the rhythm of my own beat. I played with myself until I came and then got up and pulled my sleep shorts back up. I was hoping that a good nut would help me relieve some tension, but I still felt a little tense. I went back to my cell and gathered my shower stuff, careful not to wake Trey. As I left my cell, I could feel someone watching me, although I didn't see anyone. I got naked and turned the shower on before retrieving a bucket out of the closet. I needed something to wash my clothes in. As I walked back into the shower, I could hear someone else and noticed another inmate in the shower now. I didn't know where she came from, but I asked her, "What are you doing in here so late?"

She smiled and said, "I came in here to relieve some stress." She lifted a brow and continued by saying, "I was watching you masturbate on the toilet and got turned on thinking about how good your cum would taste on my tongue."

I didn't even respond to her. I just proceeded on with my shower. I started lathering up the soap on my washcloth as she came over and grabbed it out of my hand. She reached down and opened up my pussy lips and began washing the folds of my inner lips. She then pushed me back a little and let the shower water rinse the soap off of me. She then pushed my breasts together and flicked her tongue back and forth over each nipple. "Oh, yes." She then bit each one, sending a sudden shock through my entire body.

She made sure I was rinsed off real good, and then she got the bucket, dumped out my clothes, and turned it over. She lifted up one of my legs and placed my foot on the bottom of the bucket. She then sat on the bucket and lifted my leg again, placing it over her shoulder. She had me pinned against the wall as she began kissing my thighs. She blew her hot breath on my already wet pussy, causing chills to go up my spine. She pulled back the hood on my clit and pulled it into her mouth. "Mmm." She sucked it hard and slow and then pushed two fingers inside of me. "Come on. You can do better than that. I want you to suck it harder," I said to her as I ground my pussy into her face. I gripped her hair between my fingers as I pushed her face into my folds. She pulled out her fingers, and I felt one slide into my ass. I kept telling her, "Suck this shit harder," as the water ran down my back.

I could feel something, and so I opened my eyes and saw a dark-skinned brother in a uniform, and when he noticed that I saw him, he smiled at me. He walked all the way in, and the girl between my legs stopped what she was doing. I was pissed, because I was so close to my orgasm. He told her to report back to her dormitory. At first, she looked at him crazy, but once she realized he was serious, she got dressed quickly and rushed out.

I turned the water off and grabbed my things, getting ready to leave out too. He grabbed a hold of my shoulder and stopped me. "I was doing rounds and heard the water running. Y'all ain't supposed to be in the showers this late."

I looked at him innocently and said, "I'm sorry, sir. It will never happen again." I was still naked and noticed him looking me up and down. "You see something you like, sir?"

He smiled and said in a demanding yet sexy ass voice, "I think I should check you out before you get back, so why don't you go ahead and bend over."

He didn't even give me a chance to do it before grabbing me and turning me around. I grabbed the bucket that was still there as he bent me over and pushed his dick into me. He was fucking me so good that he was lifting me up off my feet, and I was steady begging him, "Please, don't stop. Oh, yes."

He kept fucking me as my cum started squirting out all over his dick. I felt like I was gonna pass out as he suddenly pulled out of me and shot his cum all over my back while he was still cumming. I turned around and dropped to my knees so I could drink the rest of what he was serving. I swallowed what was left down my throat. When he was finished, he told me to hurry and take a shower, and then get dressed and go back to my cell. Like the good girl that I was, I did what I was told.

I made it back to my cell and quietly got in my bed. All I could think about were the orgasms I had today. I finally fell asleep and wondered what tomorrow would bring.

Chapter Twenty-Seven

I woke up the next morning and was still exhausted from the day before. I was too exhausted to even dream. I was called to the officer's station before I even got a chance to brush my teeth. I was told to go back to my cell and pack my property because I was going out to court. I guess the lawyer that Remy hired had finally gotten me a court date for a new hearing. I deserved one, because I wasn't at fault for what happened. If that truck wouldn't have come out of nowhere, I never would have had to swerve to miss it, which was what caused me to hit the guy on the bicycle. Hell, I felt like I lost more than anyone. I lost my man, my unborn child, and my freedom.

I went back to my cell and told Trey the good news. She was so happy for me too. I gave her all my food, clothes, and hygiene products and told her, "I promise, Trey. I'm gonna keep it real. You'll be out of here soon, so here's my number and address. Make sure you find me." I was hoping to see Trey in the streets because I wanted to see how she could work a real strap-on. I took only my legal papers, kissed Trey goodbye, and walked out of my cell. I was told to go to property and when I got there, I was handcuffed and shackled and put in the back of a police van so I could be taken to fight for my freedom.

It felt like the drive took forever, but it was only thirty minutes long. I was nervous and so ready to get this over with. They took me straight to the courtroom and as soon as I walked in, the first face I saw was Remy's. It had been so long since I last saw her, and my heart skipped a beat when I did. The judge came in and we all stood until told to be seated. The defense attorney Remy hired was said to be the best in the state, and I knew it was true as soon as he started his opening argument. Court lasted about an hour with each side having their turn. I didn't need a jury because it was only up to the judge to decide my fate. The judge left the courtroom for about ten minutes and then came back in to tell me my destiny. I was so nervous I felt like I was going to vomit. Tears came to my eyes as he announced for me to have time served and said that the Department of Corrections had forty-eight hours to release me. I turned around and smiled at Remy and mouthed, "Thank you" before being walked out of the courtroom. I was taken back to the prison to get my release papers signed so I could go home. I was definitely going to fuck Trey one last time before I walked out a free woman. Her sex game was on point, and I needed just one more session.

When I got back and told her what happened, she was both happy and sad. She still had a little bit of time left to do, and I promised her that I wouldn't forget her. I asked her, "Can I hit that virgin pussy one good time before I go?"

We shared a laugh before she answered me, "You damn right." That night when the cell doors closed, Trey got up and made a very small strap-on. She passed it to me and said, "This all I'm gonna be able to take."

"Don't worry, I'm gonna be very gentle." I couldn't wait any longer and was so happy that she had kept her word. She helped me put it around my hips before lying back on the bed. I went down and sucked her clit into my mouth because I wanted to get her good and wet first. I then spread her legs as wide as I could get them.

I pulled the hood from over her clit and flicked my tongue over the raw flesh. "Shit, girl. You fucking me up."

When I heard her say that, I began sucking on it and then slowly slid a finger inside of her. I moved my finger in and out real slow as she rocked her hips against the pressure of it. She was soaking wet, and I knew that it was time. I placed the tip of the strap-on at the entrance of her hole and asked, "Are you ready, Trey?"

She looked at me and only nodded her head, and then she closed her eyes. I slid into her very slow and saw her squint her eyes. I tried to ease up because I felt like I was hurting her, but she told me, "Nah, boo. Go ahead."

At about that time, I heard the cell door open and the officer that always stood at the door and watched us walked in and asked, "Y'all need some company?"

He started undoing his pants before we could even respond. Oh well, might as well go out with a bang. The officer positioned himself behind me and as I slid back into Trey, he slid into me. He rammed into me hard, causing me to do the same to Trey. She seemed to be enjoying it, so I continued to go with the flow. It didn't take the officer long before he was shooting his cum all over me. When he pulled out, I pulled out. Trey's cum covered the glove and was mixed with a little blood. It was crazy how she let me be her first. I would never forget this moment.

The night went and the day of my release was here. I was happy and couldn't wait to get home. I woke up in good spirits and was ready to live my life. I would miss Trey but would make sure that as long as she was here, she would be well taken care of. I also told her that I would put her on the lesbian website so she could accumulate some pen pals to keep her company. Trey was a good catch, and I couldn't wait for Remy to meet her. Maybe I could even talk Remy into letting her stay with us, because the three of us would make a good team. I went and said goodbye to the dark-skinned officer who I fucked in my store along with his caramel friend. I gave both of them Remy's number because I would have to get a new one. I wanted to see them in the streets too. Remy and I could share, because like me, she appreciated some good dick.

The warden summoned me to his office and gave me a number I could call him at. I threw the number back in his face and laughed while saying, "Bitch, your small ass dick won't ever grace the walls of this pussy again."

He turned red with embarrassment and hung his head low. I didn't feel bad, because it was the truth. I turned around and walked out his office and to the control room so I could go the fuck home.

Sugar E. Wallz

Chapter Twenty-Eight

I had been thinking about Remy all day and couldn't wait to see her, hold her, and most of all, taste her. There didn't seem to be any other flavor quite like hers. There was no way I could ever show her how much I appreciated what she'd done for me or even how much I cared about her. I actually had love in my heart for her, never thinking I could love a woman so much. Remy and the guy she was going to settle down with didn't work out once she miscarried his baby. For some reason, he resented her after that. It was as if he felt like she lost the baby on purpose and dumped her. Now it was up to me to help her forget and move on with her life. Remy was a strong woman, and I knew that she would be okay.

When she showed up to get me, she was as beautiful as ever. Nothing about her had changed except her thickness, which filled in the right places on her body. She brought me Versace, my favorite designer, to wear out of there. The black tank top and stretch jeans accentuated every curve in my frame. She also brought me a red bra with a thong to match. I looked damn good in my outfit, and Remy must have thought so too, from the way she was smiling. We walked out the prison gates hand in hand to a waiting stretch limo. She had gone all out for my return home. The driver had opened the back door for us, and Remy pushed me in playfully. She told the driver, "Take us home, buddy." He smiled at us through the rearview mirror and pulled away. She turned to me and asked, "Is there anywhere special you want to go?"

I kissed Remy's lips and told her, "Nah, as long as I'm with you, I'm good."

Instead of her address, the driver pulled up to the Wilshire Hotel, and I looked at Remy in amazement. This had always been my favorite hotel, and I couldn't believe that she remembered. "Oh my god, you didn't forget."

The driver got out of the car but didn't come open our door. He, instead, plopped down on the hood and just sat there. Instead of getting out of the limo, Remy told me to lie back in the seat and when I did, she removed my pants and thong but made me put my heels back on. She pulled what looked like a tube of lipstick out of her purse, and as I looked closer, I saw that it was a bullet. She asked me, "Do you want something to drink?"

I shake my head and say, "Yeah. But what I want doesn't come in one of those bottles." She laughed and then crawled up to me and gently kissed me. I heard the bullet begin buzzing and felt it hit my clit. Remy moved it up and down as my breathing escalated. She knew that this was one of my favorite toys, and if she wasn't careful, I'd cum quicker than she wanted me to.

Remy began kissing, caressing, and licking her way down each of my legs till she got to my feet. She removed a heel and sucked a toe into her mouth. She switched to the other foot and did the same, and then came back up my legs. When she got back up to my thighs, I lost all train of thought. She had always been good at sucking my pussy, and I was going crazy because it felt like she was taking forever to get to it. Then, suddenly, her teeth found my clit as she bit gently down on it. "It's about damn time," I said to her as the bullet slid into my pussy. She worked the bullet so good inside of me that my toes curled up, and then removed it and replaced it with her long tongue. "Yes, Remy, this shit feels so damn good." It felt like her tongue was touching my walls because I was so hyped up.

"Mmm," Remy moaned, and as she did, I felt the bullet enter my ass.

I could feel my orgasm building and grabbed the back of her head, pushing her into me. "Oh, Remy, I'm gonna cum, baby. Shit, I'm cumming." At about that time, my juices squirted out onto Remy's lips, and she kept going until I was completely empty. When she was done, she helped me put my clothes back on, and then I told her, "Okay, I think I'm ready for that drink now." She looked at me and we burst out laughing.

Remy knocked on the window and the limo driver opened the door, and we finally exited and went into the hotel. It was huge and more beautiful than anything I'd ever seen. I couldn't wait to get upstairs and see what our room looked like. Remy grabbed my hand and walked me to the elevator which took us to the top floor. She kissed me the whole way up, and when we made it to our suite and went inside, Remy said, "Anything for you, Nik. Anything."

I walked all the way in and saw rose petals everywhere. "Oh my god, Remy. Thank you for making this day so special," I told her as tears formed in my eyes.

She grabbed my hand and walked me to the dining room where there were two trays of food and a bottle of champagne on the oakwood table. She pulled out my chair, kissed me on the forehead, and then went to sit down. "I hope you like all of this, Nik, because I got more," she said to me, and I could feel the love in her words.

"Yes, Remy, I will never forget this."

We had filet mignon, baked potatoes, and salad with a glass of Chianti and caught up on what we had missed. "Come on, let's go take a bath together," she said as she reached out her hand.

I took it and she led me to the bathroom, and it took my breath away. It was decorated in marble shelves lined in gold. The huge hot tube was full of bubbles and a trail of roses led the path on the tiled floor. Luther Vandross was coming from the speakers that were situated on each end hanging on the wall. I turned to her and didn't even realize a tear had fallen until she wiped it from my face. "Oh, Remy, I fucking love you."

She smiled and said, "Yeah, I love you too. Now, let's not let these bubbles go to waste." We undressed and walked to the edge of the tub where Remy handed me a glass of champagne. I drank my champagne in one gulp, and Remy took the glass from my hand. I got in and she followed suit behind me. There was a bowl with strawberries covered in chocolate, and Remy began feeding them to me. She told me, "Nicole, I want to spend forever right here with you, if you let me," and then she kissed me in a way that only she could do.

She moved over and then climbed behind me, and I was now in between her legs. As she got a washcloth and squeezed the hot water down my back, I closed my eyes and told her, "Remy, I appreciate you so much and don't know what I'd do without you."

We didn't stay in the tub long and got out and dried each other off. She then took me to the bedroom where the lights were dimmed and the soft music played low. There was more champagne on the bedside table, and everything was so perfect and so beautiful. I saw a big white box sitting on the end of the bed and looked at Remy. "Well, don't just stand there looking at it. Go open it up."

I did as she said and found a satin lace teddy, and smiled. I told her, "I'll be right back." I kissed her on the cheek and then went to the bathroom to put the teddy on, and it was a perfect fit. Only Remy could know my body so well. When I walked back out, I found Remy down on one knee with a blue Tiffany box in her hand, and my hands instantly covered my face. I finally asked, "What are you doing?"

She answered me right away, "I'm trying to spend forever with you, Nik. Be my wife."

She opened the box and there sat a six-carat, emerald-cut diamond on a platinum band. I was crying hard but told her in between sobs, "Hell yeah, I'll be your wife."

She put the ring on my finger and kissed me before wiping the tears from my eyes. She walked me over to the bed and laid me down, leaving me there and walking away. When she came back, she had a bag with sex toys in it and satin straps. She took out a two-headed strap-on and some motion lotion. "Do you trust me, Nicole?" she asked me, but didn't have to because she knew I did.

I answered her anyway, "Damn right, I do." She removed the teddy off of me and climbed on the bed, blindfolding me, and then tied my arms to the bedpost. She straddled me and I could hear her remove the top off of the lotion bottle. It was cool as she rubbed it on my breasts and massaged it in, paying extra attention to my nipples. She kissed me softly on the lips and then went down and pulled a nipple into her mouth. I could feel the lotion heating up on my skin and causing a tingling effect.

She now went lower, licking down my stomach and then to my thighs. She spread my legs and opened my pussy lips. I felt her apply the lotion to my clit. As she pulled it into her mouth, it felt like it was going numb from the lotion. "Oh, Remy. Oh."

It stung but felt good at the same time as she sucked harder. She suddenly stopped, and I could feel her get off the bed, and I was lying there wondering when she was going to come back. It felt like she had been gone forever when she climbed back between my legs. I could feel the strap-on close to my holes, and she reached up and pulled the blindfold off of me. "I want to look in your eyes while I make you feel good," she told me as the two-headed strap-on entered me, opening up both holes.

"Shit, Remy. Fuck me, baby. Yes." She fucked me long and hard and didn't let up until I told her, "I'm cumming, Remy."

She then slowed down as my pussy juice covered the strap-on. As she untied my hands, she said, "We ain't done yet."

We got in a sixty-nine position and I was so excited because I'd always loved the taste of her pussy. We came in each other's mouths and just lay there without moving for a little while before finally falling asleep, exhausted from the events we shared.

Sugar E. Wallz

Chapter Twenty-Nine

It was kinda nice waking up to Remy every morning, although I did miss my morning masturbation session. Now, instead of fucking myself, Remy and I fucked each other. Remy's pussy tasted even sweeter after marinating all night. I happened to wake up a little earlier than usual and looked over at Remy's naked body lying next to me. The sheet was down just enough to see her perky little nipples poking out, looking at me. I reached over and pinched it really hard, waking her. "Ouch," she yelled as she slapped my hand away and then started laughing.

I didn't let that stop me, so I propped myself up on one elbow and sucked it into my mouth and flicked my tongue over it. I pulled the sheet all the way off of her as I felt her hand brace the back of my head. "Mmm, hmm," I heard her moaning from the sensation. I peeked up at her and saw a smile grace her beautiful face. I came up and went to her mouth and traced the lining of her lips before we started kissing. I was trying to get used to this, but there was no way it could ever stop me from wanting dick. I mean, the strap-on was good, but I loved the feel of a man's chest when he was on top of me. Nothing else could compare to that.

I slowly licked all the way down to her navel, and as I got lower, her legs spread naturally. Her pussy was so pretty and smelled so sweet. I opened the lips and saw her juices covering her hole while some was draining down her asshole. I took my tongue and licked them off of her. I then slowly inserted a finger into her as I pulled her swollen clit into my mouth. "Sss, yes, Nicole," she said as I sucked harder.

She pulled my hair and a slight moan escaped me. "Mmm, mmm."

The harder I sucked, the harder she pulled and the more she rolled her hips into my face. I pushed and pulled my fingers in and out of her, but I didn't want her to cum yet, so I slowed down and then pulled them out. I heard Remy cuss and ask, "Shit. What the fuck?"

She didn't say anything else once she saw the dildo in my hand. Instead, she smiled at me and reached down to spread her lips. Remy was always ready for a good fuck, and I was anxious to deliver. I looked at her and just shook my head, and she knew what I wanted her to do. She turned around and got on all fours and arched her back to where her ass and pussy were sitting up looking at me. "That's a good girl," I said as I got behind her and spread her ass cheeks to open her pussy up. I placed the head of the strap-on at her hole and guided it gently inside, her juices gushing out on the sides of it. As I went in and out of her, she reached down and began playing with her own clit. "You like this, Remy?" I asked her, because I loved it when she talked to me.

She answered, "Yes. Fuck me harder, bitch." I fucked her with a force I didn't know I had in me, and our skin was meeting and making a clapping sound. Her ass was jiggling like a pool of waves, I was fucking her so hard. "I'm gonna cum, Nicole. Fuck me, baby, I'm gonna cum."

The strap-on was rubbing against my clit, causing a reaction with her, as Remy's cum covered the dick. I squirted at the same time but kept my pace in her pussy. I was weakening from my orgasm and covered in sweat as I started slowing down. I could feel my cum running down my leg and began to wish that I had time to let her fuck me too. However, I still worked for Jamal and had to get ready for work. I figured I could just wait until I got there and let Jamal do what Remy didn't. I finally pulled out of her and went to get in the shower while she stayed in the bed. She had to work tonight, so she would need her rest. I planned on showering up and watching her like it was my first time.

As I was washing my hair, I felt someone between my legs, spreading my pussy. Remy was there, and I told her, "You know I don't have time for this." However, I did nothing to stop her as I placed my palm on one wall and my other one on the top of her head. I couldn't resist her touch no matter what I did. The water splashing on my face didn't stop me from riding her and meeting her rhythm. I took one leg and placed it on the ledge as she sucked my pussy hard and fast. "Oh, Remy," I called her name, but it's Robert I'm thinking about once again.

I still missed him. No matter how hard I tried to move on, his memory would never leave me. Thinking of him made me cum even quicker and made me feel guilty, but I kept it to myself. I got dressed and when I made it to the office, I walked in and straight to my desk, as if I wasn't fifteen minutes late. "Damn, Remy," I said to myself.

Not even a minute later, Jamal summoned me to his office. When I walked in, Jamal was sitting behind his desk, and to my surprise, the security officer was standing by the window. I didn't know what the hell was going on, so I just stood there. Jamal stared at me and then rose to his feet and asked, "You feel like having some fun?"

He got close enough to me that I could feel his hot breath on my skin, and I answered, "I'm always down for a good time."

The security officer walked over to me next and got behind me. Jamal unbuttoned my blouse as the security officer unzipped my pencil skirt, and it instantly fell to my feet. My nipples rose and my pussy got wet. The officer then unsnapped my bra as Jamal pulled my panties down. I was left with only my six-inch heels on my feet. I was being violated in the best way, and it made me regret my decision to marry a woman. How did I possibly think I could be without a man's touch?

My clit was pulsing so hard I thought that it was about to burst. I had my eyes closed when I felt both of them pull away from me. I opened my eyes and saw that they were only getting undressed. As soon as they were naked, they were back on me. I reached out in front of me and gripped their dicks, one in each hand. Both filled my hand to capacity as I started stroking them. I felt their pre-cum in my hand and rubbed it in like lotion.

"Spread them legs for me," Jamal said as he dropped to his knees.

He spread my pussy lips as the officer spread my ass cheeks. Jamal sucked my clit into his mouth and I felt the officer drop down and began licking my asshole. I then felt each of them glide a finger inside of me. "Oh my god, I am so fucking wet," I told them as I got a head rush. I wasn't sure how much more I could take, so I said three words, "Please, fuck me."

Jamal walked away and got a blanket out of his filing cabinet and spread it on the floor. All I could think about was these two dicks running up inside of me. It had been a minute since I had some good dick, so I was good and ready.

I got on all fours while Jamal got behind me and the officer got in front of me on his knees. As I sucked the officer's dick into my mouth, Jamal slowly entered me. I arched my back so he could go deeper. "Suck that dick good for me," the officer told me as I felt Jamal's balls slamming into my clit.

I slammed back into him as the officer gripped my hair and shoved his dick deep into my mouth. After a few minutes, Jamal pulled out of me and told me to stand up. I let the dick fall out of my mouth and did as he said. The officer then lay down on the blanket and held his erect dick in his hand to where it was pointing straight in the air. Jamal came behind me and said, "Sit on his dick and ride it."

I straddled the officer and then squatted down, tooting my ass up high and letting Jamal slide his dick into my ass. The officer's dick felt bigger this time, but I wasn't complaining. Slowly, in and out, the double penetration brought me pleasure. "You like all this dick in you, Nicole?" Jamal asked as he went inside of me hard.

I answered between thrusts, "Yes. Oh, Yes. I-I-love-this-shit." I felt the officer reach down and pull on my clit, and it gave me a rush. I knew that I was about to cum. "I'm gonna cum," I blurted out right before I squirted all over the officer's dick. They both then pulled out of me and jacked their dicks as cum began shooting out. I went from one to the other, licking and sucking off as much as I possibly could. When we were done, we got dressed and then went about our day as if nothing ever happened.

I spent the rest of my day catching up on reports that were long overdue. All while sitting there with cum-soaked panties on, my pussy still felt the after effects of Jamal and the officer, and all I could think about was telling Remy that I missed a real dick from a real man. I knew that it was going to break her heart, but I missed my single life and really didn't want to be tied down or obligated to anyone. Losing Robert made me even more vulnerable and caused me to move too quickly.

It was late when I left work, and I knew that Remy would already be gone. I figured I should go home and wash the cum off of me before going to the club where she was. It was nice coming home and being able to relax and be alone for a while. I kicked off my heels and took off everything but my thong. I got me something to drink and sat on the couch so I could get my thoughts together. The drink gave me a slight buzz, and even though sex wasn't on my mind, I reached up and started playing with my nipples. I pushed a breast up to my mouth and sucked a nipple between my lips. I flicked my tongue over it a few times before switching to the other one.

My legs began to spread, as if on cue, and I reached down and pushed a finger into my pussy. My thong was in the way so I pulled out, took them off, and then went back in. As I moved my finger in and out, I thought of Robert and the feeling that his dick gave me. My finger was coated with my juice when I pulled it out, and I put it in my mouth and sucked it off. I went back down and started pulling on my clit and then massaging it in slow circular movements. I began to press harder and move quicker as I called Robert's name, "Oh, Robert, baby. My god, I miss you." It only took me a couple of minutes to cum, and when I finished, I finally got up and went to take my shower so I could get dressed and go break the news to Remy.

The club was packed, as always, and, of course, I walked past the entire line and went to the front. The bouncer smiled as I walked past him and reached out to feel the dick. "Evening, ma'am."

I went to the bouncer by the stage and asked about Remy, "Has she gone on yet?"

He looked me up and down and smiled before saying, "Nah, lil' mama, she goes on next."

I winked at him and said "Thank you" before grabbing a seat at the bottom of the stage. When she came out on stage, she didn't come alone but instead, had another dancer with her. I watched as they shook their asses together and about two minutes into their set, Remy noticed me. She shook her head at the other dancer, and they started undressing. The other dancer then stood behind Remy and reached down to spread her pussy lips open for the whole club to see. Her clit poked out and was rock hard and swollen. I was getting turned on, and it was as if Remy knew it, because she nodded her head at me to join them. The bouncer helped me up on the stage and I undressed before kneeling down in front of my wife. As she turned her head to kiss the dancer behind her, I sucked her clit into my mouth. I slowly flicked my tongue over it as she rotated her wide hips. Her pussy tasted like fresh strawberries. The club was hyped up from watching our little show. I sucked on Remy's clit hard and while doing so, I could feel my ass being lifted.

I didn't even turn around to see who was behind me, but I felt it when he entered me. The dick that went in me felt so big I thought I had been split open. However, I took it like a good girl and moaned in pleasure as he slid in and out of my pussy like he had been there before. He eventually was slamming into me so hard that I had to let go of Remy's clit. Even though the club music was loud, I could still hear his body slamming into mine. He fucked me long and hard until he finally pulled out and shot his cum all over all three of us. I didn't know who he was, but the dick was so good that I was determined to find out.

There was no way that I could take anything more tonight, so I got dressed and told Remy that I would see her when she got home.

Chapter Thirty

While lying next to Remy that night, I drifted off into a deep sleep and began dreaming. I could feel him walk into the room. I knew it was him without even looking. His presence was always so fierce and so strong. The closer he got, the stronger his aroma became and the wetter my pussy became. I almost stopped breathing when he climbed in the bed beside me. I turned to face him and he instantly sucked my bottom lip into his mouth and then kissed me. His kiss was so passionate you would have thought the room would catch on fire. We stopped kissing and he ran his tongue from my mouth to my neck and then down to my breasts.

His tongue then traced the circle around my nipples before running over their hardness. He reached up and tugged on the one he was not licking. Pulling on it as if he was trying to pull it off. He switched, giving the other one the same attention. I ran my hand over his dark waves. His dreads were gone now and I missed them, but loved the new look. He went to my navel and licked around it before going lower. As he licked the length of my pussy lips, I moaned in pleasure, "Mmm, ooh."

My clit peeked out at him as my legs opened wider. His long finger found my wetness and dove in like it was a swimming pool as he sucked my clit into his warm mouth. He sucked slowly, all the while using his fingers to fill my walls, hitting every side in a way that only he could manage. I rocked my hips back and forth to enhance the feeling he was giving me. His tongue did somersaults over my clit as he continued to suck it. A technique only he could master. I took my small hands and placed them on my breasts, caressing them and twisting my nipples between my fingers. I pressed them hard and pulled on them. I felt myself ready to cum, and Robert could feel it too, because he knew my body better than I did.

He stopped sucking my clit and pulled his finger out of me. He lifted my legs and pushed them to my shoulders, placing me in the buck position, one of my favorites. He put the head to my entrance and it glided in because it knew where home was. My legs were all the way back as he went deep. Deeper than anyone else had ever gone. I looked down and watched as his dick went in and out of me. It disappeared in my depths and then reappeared again, his balls slapping against my ass cheeks as I grabbed him and pulled him deeper. I could feel the pressure all the way up to my chest and told him, "Fuck me, Robert. Yes, baby, fuck me."

He began fucking me harder, as if he was angry, and who knows, maybe he was. Maybe he was mad about me moving on without him.

I could hear our bodies colliding. Sweat was dripping from him onto me. I ran my hands over his sculpted chest and felt myself about to cum. He didn't stop this time because he had also reached his peak. No one had ever made me cum the same way he did. He pushed into me harder as my cum coated his beautiful black dick and ran down to my ass. He slowed so I could enjoy this moment, and to stop himself from cumming. He wasn't ready. Just a little more and he would be. He pulled out of me and lay on his back, and I got up and mounted him backwards.

As he disappeared inside of me, I could feel his hands spread my ass cheeks, and then he slid his thumb inside. I grabbed onto his balls and massaged them as I rode him. The pressure from his thumb brought me extra pleasure, and as I slammed onto him, my ass jiggled. I felt him pulse and knew that he was ready now. Ready to fill me with all of his love, and I was ready too. I reached lower and slid a finger into his ass, and as soon as I did, he gripped my ass cheeks hard and shot his seeds into me, filling my walls. I loved that I had the ability to make him cum this hard. I was suddenly jerked awake and looked for him lying next to me, but he was gone. Instead, I saw Remy looking at me. "What's wrong, Nik?" she asked as a tear fell from my eyes.

I lied and told her, "Nothing, Remy, it was just a bad dream." I knew that I didn't have to lie to her, but at that moment, it was all I could do. I didn't want to add any more heartbreak because tomorrow, I would tell her that I wanted out. I didn't want to be tied down to one person. I hoped she would understand.

It was beginning to be a little awkward around the condo, so we decided that it would be best if one of us moved out. Remy decided that she would go stay with one of the other dancers to make things easier. It was the best decision we would ever make. However, we both knew that we would have a friend forever. Early one morning, my doorbell rang and I got up to find Jamal at my door. Jamal came to tell me about a prosperous business venture that he came across. I asked him, "Why wouldn't you just call or wait until I come in?"

He said, "Because this just couldn't wait," as he unzipped his zipper. I was always down to fuck Jamal, so I reached into the open hole and pulled out his dick. I ran my long fingernails over his skin and watched as it slowly grew long and hard. I bent over and licked from the bottom of the shaft to the head, and then circled my tongue around it before licking the pre-cum off the tip. Jamal then sat on the couch and leaned his head back as I dropped to my knees. He put both of his hands on the back of my head and pushed. The more he pushed, the deeper his dick went down my throat, my gag reflex on full alert.

I came back up and stayed on the head for a minute before going all the way back down again. I then let it fall all the way out and pulled his pants the rest of the way off of him. I spread his legs slightly apart and sucked his balls into my wet mouth and heard him say, "Damn, I love it when you do that shit." I sucked hard as I slipped a finger up his ass and then used my free hand to jack his dick. The pressure in his ass and the pressure from sucking his balls at the same time had him ready to cum. "Damn it, I'm about to cum already," he told me as I came off of his balls and took his dick back into my mouth.

As soon as I did, I felt his warm juice hit the back of my throat, and I swallowed until each and every drop was gone. Just then, the doorbell rang, and since I wasn't expecting anybody, I wondered who it was. I looked out the peephole and was surprised to find Trey, my cellmate from prison. I opened the door with excitement and pulled her into a tight hug. "Oh my god, is it really you?"

I couldn't believe it. I invited her in and she froze when she saw Jamal sitting on the couch with his pants around his ankles and his dick in his hand. I thought she would turn around and leave, but instead, she started stripping and said, "Looks like I got here just in time."

I started kissing her and then sucked on her nipples and told her, "I want to see that dick inside of this pussy." As I rubbed on her clit, Jamal just sat back and watched as I sucked her nipples one at a time into my mouth. I reached down between her legs and slid a finger into her, pulling it in and out a couple of times before putting it in my mouth and sucking her juices off of it. I stuck my finger back into her, and when I pulled it out this time, I stuck it into her own mouth. I then walked her over to the couch where Jamal was and had her sit on him backwards. I grabbed his dick and slapped her pussy with it a couple of times before taking it back in my mouth. I saw Jamal's hands come around and start playing with her clit. He made small circular movements as she moaned in delight. "Mmm, that feels so good."

I told her to sit up a little, and as Jamal began playing with her nipples, I put the head of his dick at her entrance and told her to slide down. She went down slowly, and I saw her tense up for a second from the girth of him. I pulled her clit into my mouth, hoping that it would make it easier for her, and after a few seconds, she was at ease. I got up and went to the back of the couch and sat my pussy over Jamal's face. This nigga was freaky as fuck and had no limits when it came to sex. I rode his face while Trey rode his dick. As I came, I smeared my juices into his face with my pussy, and when Jamal was about to cum, he pushed Trey off of him, and she turned around and took him into her mouth just in time.

When Jamal left, Trey and I chilled for a little while, enjoying each other's company and catching up on each other's lives. We talked so long that I didn't even remember falling asleep, but when I woke up, Trey was gone and a note was on the coffee table with her number. She told me there was a party later and invited me and made sure to write, "wear something black." I was curious, so, of course, I was going. When I got there, I was led into the house by a woman in six-inch black heels and a pair of black panties. Her pussy lips were hanging out because there was no crotch in the panties. Her clit peeked out too, and had a small circular ring attached to it.

She had barbells pierced through her large nipples and a leather strap in her hand. I remembered this kind of shit from the BDSM party but still couldn't turn away. I didn't see Trey anywhere but was so amazed by this woman in front of me that I didn't care.

Two men approached me and told me that I needed to strip to stay. I was about to protest until Trey walked up and told them I was with her. She helped me get undressed and called the two men back. They each grabbed a leg and lifted me, carrying me over to a chair with a big hole in the seat. They then spread my legs, and each one took a pussy lip and pulled, and my clit popped out with excitement. This shit was weird, but the anticipation was killing me. The girl in the crotchless panties approached me. She had a long pink dildo in her hand that looked like it would bust me open. The men each took a finger and began massaging my clit at the same time. I suddenly felt the dildo go inside of me, and it didn't hurt like I thought it would. The woman was actually very gentle. I then felt the chair vibrate and out of nowhere, something entered my ass. "Oh, shit."

Trey came over and pinched my nipples while the strangers fucked me into submission. I was feeling sensations in places I had never felt before. I came really fast and really hard. My cum squirted all over the pink dildo and when I was done, the female licked off every drop. It was a lot to take in, but I must admit that I did enjoy myself. I didn't stay too long after that, because I started thinking of Remy and figured I'd go see her one last time.

When I walked in the club, I was told that Remy was in her dressing room, so that's where I went. I opened her door slowly because I could hear moaning. I didn't want to fuck up her groove. My pussy got wet when I looked at the scene in front of me. I saw Remy's legs wrapped around the waist of the bouncer as he had her back to the wall. The muscles in his ass cheeks flexed every time he pushed into her. Remy's eyes were closed, but I knew she felt my presence. I put a lone finger to my lips, telling her not to say anything as I crept in.

I got behind the bouncer and ran a finger down his ass crack. He didn't even break his rhythm. I put my hand between his legs and gently pulled on his balls before dropping to my knees and spreading his ass cheeks. I flicked my tongue over his asshole and traced its outline. He smelled fresh and clean. He started ramming into Remy even harder and then pulled out quickly, cumming all over her stomach. When he pulled his dick out, it was enormous and I wondered how Remy could take so much dick. I pushed him to the side and began kissing Remy as he stood there rubbing on his dick. I turned to him and said, "Nah, buddy, the party's over."

Remy looked at him, shrugged her shoulders, and giggled. He looked disappointed as he walked out, leaving me and Remy alone. I spent a little time with her and then went home and went straight to bed.

Once again, I went into a dream, and Robert was there laying on the left side of me. I was clothed only in my birthday suit. He was caressing, lightly touching, squeezing, and pinching my exposed nipples. My breathing became heavier, and I moved over and pressed my body against his. I turned my back to him and his hardness pressed against my ass cheeks. I could feel his pre-cum on my ass as a light breeze flowed over the wetness. We were so in sync that no words needed to be spoken. I knew that I could relax and enjoy him because he had my pussy trained so well.

The shift in my body exposed my most vulnerable parts, and I spread my left leg and hooked it over him. I took one of his hands and sucked on his fingers as if they were his dick. He pushed on my clit and then glided his manhood inside of me. I breathed heavier and could see my breasts rise and fall. I pulled on my nipples as he went in and out of me and stroked my clit faster. He then pulled out, but only long enough to get on top of me and re-enter. I was ready to cum but I was trying not to because I wanted this feeling to last. His dick filled my inner walls, and I could feel the orgasm steady building and couldn't hold it anymore.

I finally let it go and squirted cum all over his dick. It was now covered in my juices as he pulled out of me and lay on his back. I got up and mounted him so I could give him the same pleasure. I swore I could feel him all in my chest as I rode him to the point of no return until his seeds ignited my insides. I got off of him and a tear dropped from my eyes. As he wiped it away, I woke up and could still feel the wetness on my face. I still couldn't believe that he was gone and wondered if he was ever going to let me move on. I knew that I could never share with another what I shared with him. I tried to have it with Remy, but it just wasn't the same. I lay there for a while in the quiet of the night until I finally went back to sleep.

Sugar E. Wallz

Chapter Thirty-One

I got up the next day and told myself that today I was quitting my job and moving away from here. I felt like a change of scenery may do me some good and hopefully help me move past Robert's memory. As of now, everything reminded me of him, but I had to go see Remy first and tell her goodbye. I also wanted to spend some time with the bouncer from the club. I pulled up to the club and lo and behold, the bouncer was there getting out of his car. We were both parked in the back, so no one saw us. I told him that I wanted him to bend me over his car and fuck me like I did something wrong. He was amazed by my boldness.

He grabbed my arm and pushed me onto the hood of his car and pulled my pants down to my ankles. The hood of his car was still warm and felt good against my skin. He showed me no mercy as he rammed his dick into me. He did it with so much force I almost lost my breath. "Fuck me harder," I told him, as I felt a sudden slap on my ass cheeks that left a stinging sensation. I pulled my arms back and grabbed my own ass cheeks, pulling them apart as far as they would go. "Fuck me harder, dammit."

His body slammed into me harder and I could hear him panting. I felt him speed up and then he pulled out and came all between my ass cheeks. I turned around and looked him in the eyes, and with no words said, it's as if he understood me. He picked me up and sat me on the hood of the car, and then bent down, burying his face in my pussy. He sucked my clit slow and then sped up. It didn't take me long to cum all over his mouth and chin, and I was finally satisfied. When we were done, we fixed our clothes and walked away as if nothing happened. I proceeded into the club to do one of the hardest things I'd ever done.

They told me that Remy didn't come in that night, so I left and went to her apartment. When I got there, I stayed in my car for a few minutes before getting out and knocking on the door. When Remy opened it, she had on a bath towel around her and nothing else. Droplets of water clung to her skin, as if they were afraid to let go. When she saw me, she instantly dropped the towel to the floor and pulled me in. It was as if she already knew what I was there for. She kissed me, and I could feel the intensity of it. When we stopped kissing, I got undressed and she led me to the couch.

I started to speak, but she held her hand over my mouth to stop me. I submitted to her demand and then went straight to her nipples. I sucked each one before she pushed me away and then attacked mine with her long pink tongue. I then lay back as she parted my pussy lips with her small hands and started playing with my clit. As she sucked on it, I closed my eyes and enjoyed the feeling. She stuck her tongue in my pussy as far as it would go and then pushed a finger into my ass. While she was eating me, I told her how much she meant to me and apologized for all I put her through. She was eating me so good until all of my emotions began pouring out.

I grinded into her face as she sucked my clit back into her mouth. I twisted my nipples as she brought me to ecstasy. After I came, we got in the scissors position and rubbed our clits together until we were done. We lay there reminiscing about all we had been through. We said what needed to be said to each other so that we could both start new chapters in our lives. My love for Remy was deep, but it didn't fill me like the love I had for Robert. I told her that I didn't know where I was going yet. I only knew that I needed to go. I ended up falling asleep in Remy's arms, still wet from our little rendezvous. When I woke up the next morning, she was already gone. She left a note saying it would be easier if she wasn't there when I left, and, of course, I understood. I knew that she would miss me, but I hoped that one day she'd find what she needed to fill her heart. I, myself, didn't even know what I would find or even if I would find anything at all. I just knew I needed to go. I got up, took a shower, and went to tie up a few more loose ends before I would begin my journey.

Epilogue

I decided to just travel, never settling in one place too long. I had worked long and hard and had enough money saved to take care of myself for a while. I missed Remy and Jamal but enjoyed my new-found freedom. One day, I would make my way back and revisit what I left behind. But for now, I was enjoying me. I still loved to fuck and would go to different strip clubs to find me a flavor for the night. Sometimes, I even took two. I also ran into a few niggas with some good dick for a one-night stand. I guess some things would never change.

Submission Guideline

Submit the first three chapters of your completed manuscript to ldpsubmissions@gmail.com, subject line: Your book's title. The manuscript must be in a .doc file and sent as an attachment. Document should be in Times New Roman, double spaced and in size 12 font. Also, provide your synopsis and full contact information. If sending multiple submissions, they must each be in a separate email.

Have a story but no way to send it electronically? You can still submit to LDP/Ca$h Presents. Send in the first three chapters, written or typed, of your completed manuscript to:

LDP: Submissions Dept
Po Box 944
Stockbridge, Ga 30281

DO NOT send original manuscript. Must be a duplicate.

Provide your synopsis and a cover letter containing your full contact information.

Thanks for considering LDP and Ca$h Presents.

Coming Soon from Lock Down Publications/Ca$h Presents

BOW DOWN TO MY GANGSTA

By **Ca$h**

TORN BETWEEN TWO

By **Coffee**

THE STREETS STAINED MY SOUL **II**

By **Marcellus Allen**

BLOOD OF A BOSS **VI**

SHADOWS OF THE GAME II

TRAP BASTARD II

By **Askari**

LOYAL TO THE GAME **IV**

By **T.J. & Jelissa**

IF LOVING YOU IS WRONG... **III**

By **Jelissa**

TRUE SAVAGE **VIII**

MIDNIGHT CARTEL IV

DOPE BOY MAGIC IV

CITY OF KINGZ III

By **Chris Green**

BLAST FOR ME **III**

A SAVAGE DOPEBOY III

CUTTHROAT MAFIA III

DUFFLE BAG CARTEL VI

HEARTLESS GOON VI

By **Ghost**

A HUSTLER'S DECEIT III

KILL ZONE **II**

BAE BELONGS TO ME III

A DOPE BOY'S QUEEN III

By **Aryanna**

COKE KINGS V

KING OF THE TRAP III

By **T.J. Edwards**

GORILLAZ IN THE BAY V

3X KRAZY III

De'Kari

THE STREETS ARE CALLING II

Duquie Wilson

KINGPIN KILLAZ IV

STREET KINGS III

PAID IN BLOOD III

CARTEL KILLAZ IV

DOPE GODS III

Hood Rich

SINS OF A HUSTLA II

ASAD

KINGZ OF THE GAME VI

Playa Ray

SLAUGHTER GANG IV

RUTHLESS HEART IV

By Willie Slaughter

FUK SHYT II

By Blakk Diamond

TRAP QUEEN

RICH $AVAGE II

By Troublesome

YAYO V

GHOST MOB II

Stilloan Robinson
CREAM III
By Yolanda Moore
SON OF A DOPE FIEND III
HEAVEN GOT A GHETTO II
By Renta
FOREVER GANGSTA II
GLOCKS ON SATIN SHEETS III
By Adrian Dulan
LOYALTY AIN'T PROMISED III
By Keith Williams
THE PRICE YOU PAY FOR LOVE III
By Destiny Skai
I'M NOTHING WITHOUT HIS LOVE II
SINS OF A THUG II
By Monet Dragun
LIFE OF A SAVAGE IV
MURDA SEASON IV
GANGLAND CARTEL IV
CHI'RAQ GANGSTAS IV
KILLERS ON ELM STREET III
JACK BOYZ N DA BRONX II
A DOPEBOY'S DREAM II
By Romell Tukes
QUIET MONEY IV
EXTENDED CLIP III
THUG LIFE IV
By Trai'Quan
THE STREETS MADE ME III

Sugar E. Wallz

By **Larry D. Wright**
IF YOU CROSS ME ONCE II
ANGEL III
By **Anthony Fields**
FRIEND OR FOE III
By **Mimi**
SAVAGE STORMS III
By **Meesha**
BLOOD ON THE MONEY III
By J-Blunt
THE STREETS WILL NEVER CLOSE II
By K'ajji
NIGHTMARES OF A HUSTLA III
By King Dream
IN THE ARM OF HIS BOSS
By Jamila
MONEY, MURDER & MEMORIES III
Malik D. Rice
CONCRETE KILLAZ II
By Kingpen
HARD AND RUTHLESS II
By Von Wiley Hall
LEVELS TO THIS SHYT II
By Ah'Million
MOB TIES II
By SayNoMore
BODYMORE MURDERLAND II
By Delmont Player
THE LAST OF THE OGS III
Tranay Adams

166

FOR THE LOVE OF A BOSS II
By C. D. Blue

Available Now

RESTRAINING ORDER **I & II**
By **CA$H & Coffee**
LOVE KNOWS NO BOUNDARIES **I II & III**
By **Coffee**
RAISED AS A GOON I, II, III & IV
BRED BY THE SLUMS I, II, III
BLAST FOR ME I & II
ROTTEN TO THE CORE I II III
A BRONX TALE I, II, III
DUFFLE BAG CARTEL I II III IV V
HEARTLESS GOON I II III IV V
A SAVAGE DOPEBOY I II
DRUG LORDS I II III
CUTTHROAT MAFIA I II
By **Ghost**
LAY IT DOWN **I & II**
LAST OF A DYING BREED I II
BLOOD STAINS OF A SHOTTA I & II III
By **Jamaica**
LOYAL TO THE GAME I II III
LIFE OF SIN I, II III
By **TJ & Jelissa**
BLOODY COMMAS I & II

SKI MASK CARTEL I II & III

KING OF NEW YORK I II,III IV V

RISE TO POWER I II III

COKE KINGS I II III IV

BORN HEARTLESS I II III IV

KING OF THE TRAP I II

By **T.J. Edwards**

IF LOVING HIM IS WRONG...I & II

LOVE ME EVEN WHEN IT HURTS I II III

By **Jelissa**

WHEN THE STREETS CLAP BACK I & II III

THE HEART OF A SAVAGE I II III

By **Jibril Williams**

A DISTINGUISHED THUG STOLE MY HEART I II & III

LOVE SHOULDN'T HURT I II III IV

RENEGADE BOYS I II III IV

PAID IN KARMA I II III

SAVAGE STORMS I II

By **Meesha**

A GANGSTER'S CODE I &, II III

A GANGSTER'S SYN I II III

THE SAVAGE LIFE I II III

CHAINED TO THE STREETS I II III

BLOOD ON THE MONEY I II

By J-Blunt

PUSH IT TO THE LIMIT

By **Bre' Hayes**

BLOOD OF A BOSS **I, II, III, IV, V**

SHADOWS OF THE GAME

TRAP BASTARD

Cum for Me 7

By **Askari**
THE STREETS BLEED MURDER **I, II & III**
THE HEART OF A GANGSTA I II& III
By **Jerry Jackson**
CUM FOR ME I II III IV V VI VII
An **LDP Erotica Collaboration**
BRIDE OF A HUSTLA **I II & II**
THE FETTI GIRLS **I, II& III**
CORRUPTED BY A GANGSTA I, II III, IV
BLINDED BY HIS LOVE
THE PRICE YOU PAY FOR LOVE I II
DOPE GIRL MAGIC I II III
By **Destiny Skai**
WHEN A GOOD GIRL GOES BAD
By **Adrienne**
THE COST OF LOYALTY I II III
By Kweli
A GANGSTER'S REVENGE **I II III & IV**
THE BOSS MAN'S DAUGHTERS I II III IV V
A SAVAGE LOVE **I & II**
BAE BELONGS TO ME I II
A HUSTLER'S DECEIT I, II, III
WHAT BAD BITCHES DO I, II, III
SOUL OF A MONSTER I II III
KILL ZONE
A DOPE BOY'S QUEEN I II
By **Aryanna**
A KINGPIN'S AMBITON
A KINGPIN'S AMBITION **II**
I MURDER FOR THE DOUGH

Sugar E. Wallz

By **Ambitious**
TRUE SAVAGE I II III IV V VI VII
DOPE BOY MAGIC I, II, III
MIDNIGHT CARTEL I II III
CITY OF KINGZ I II
By **Chris Green**
A DOPEBOY'S PRAYER
By **Eddie "Wolf" Lee**
THE KING CARTEL **I, II & III**
By **Frank Gresham**
THESE NIGGAS AIN'T LOYAL **I, II & III**
By **Nikki Tee**
GANGSTA SHYT **I II &III**
By **CATO**
THE ULTIMATE BETRAYAL
By **Phoenix**
BOSS'N UP **I , II & III**
By **Royal Nicole**
I LOVE YOU TO DEATH
By Destiny J
I RIDE FOR MY HITTA
I STILL RIDE FOR MY HITTA
By **Misty Holt**
LOVE & CHASIN' PAPER
By **Qay Crockett**
TO DIE IN VAIN
SINS OF A HUSTLA
By **ASAD**
BROOKLYN HUSTLAZ
By **Boogsy Morina**

BROOKLYN ON LOCK I & II

By **Sonovia**

GANGSTA CITY

By **Teddy Duke**

A DRUG KING AND HIS DIAMOND I & II III

A DOPEMAN'S RICHES

HER MAN, MINE'S TOO I, II

CASH MONEY HO'S

THE WIFEY I USED TO BE I II

By Nicole Goosby

TRAPHOUSE KING **I II & III**

KINGPIN KILLAZ I II III

STREET KINGS I II

PAID IN BLOOD **I II**

CARTEL KILLAZ I II III

DOPE GODS I II

By **Hood Rich**

LIPSTICK KILLAH **I, II, III**

CRIME OF PASSION I II & III

FRIEND OR FOE I II

By **Mimi**

STEADY MOBBN' **I, II, III**

THE STREETS STAINED MY SOUL

By **Marcellus Allen**

WHO SHOT YA **I, II, III**

SON OF A DOPE FIEND I II

HEAVEN GOT A GHETTO

Renta

GORILLAZ IN THE BAY **I II III IV**

TEARS OF A GANGSTA I II

3X KRAZY I II

DE'KARI

TRIGGADALE I II III

Elijah R. Freeman

GOD BLESS THE TRAPPERS I, II, III

THESE SCANDALOUS STREETS I, II, III

FEAR MY GANGSTA I, II, III IV, V

THESE STREETS DON'T LOVE NOBODY I, II

BURY ME A G I, II, III, IV, V

A GANGSTA'S EMPIRE I, II, III, IV

THE DOPEMAN'S BODYGAURD I II

THE REALEST KILLAZ I II III

THE LAST OF THE OGS I II

Tranay Adams

THE STREETS ARE CALLING

Duquie Wilson

MARRIED TO A BOSS… I II III

By Destiny Skai & Chris Green

KINGZ OF THE GAME I II III IV V

Playa Ray

SLAUGHTER GANG I II III

RUTHLESS HEART I II III

By Willie Slaughter

FUK SHYT

By Blakk Diamond

DON'T F#CK WITH MY HEART I II

By Linnea

ADDICTED TO THE DRAMA I II III

IN THE ARM OF HIS BOSS II

By Jamila

YAYO I II III IV

A SHOOTER'S AMBITION I II

By S. Allen

TRAP GOD I II III

RICH $AVAGE

By Troublesome

FOREVER GANGSTA

GLOCKS ON SATIN SHEETS I II

By Adrian Dulan

TOE TAGZ I II III

LEVELS TO THIS SHYT

By Ah'Million

KINGPIN DREAMS I II III

By Paper Boi Rari

CONFESSIONS OF A GANGSTA I II III

By Nicholas Lock

I'M NOTHING WITHOUT HIS LOVE

SINS OF A THUG

By Monet Dragun

CAUGHT UP IN THE LIFE I II III

By Robert Baptiste

NEW TO THE GAME I II III

MONEY, MURDER & MEMORIES I II

By **Malik D. Rice**

LIFE OF A SAVAGE I II III

A GANGSTA'S QUR'AN I II III

MURDA SEASON I II III

GANGLAND CARTEL I II III

CHI'RAQ GANGSTAS I II III

KILLERS ON ELM STREET I II

JACK BOYZ N DA BRONX

A DOPEBOY'S DREAM

By **Romell Tukes**

LOYALTY AIN'T PROMISED I II

By Keith Williams

QUIET MONEY I II III

THUG LIFE I II III

EXTENDED CLIP I II

By **Trai'Quan**

THE STREETS MADE ME I II

By **Larry D. Wright**

THE ULTIMATE SACRIFICE I, II, III, IV, V, VI

KHADIFI

IF YOU CROSS ME ONCE

ANGEL I II

By **Anthony Fields**

THE LIFE OF A HOOD STAR

By Ca$h & Rashia Wilson

THE STREETS WILL NEVER CLOSE

By K'ajji

CREAM I II

By Yolanda Moore

NIGHTMARES OF A HUSTLA I II

By King Dream

CONCRETE KILLAZ

By Kingpen

HARD AND RUTHLESS

By Von Wiley Hall

GHOST MOB II

Stilloan Robinson
MOB TIES
By SayNoMore
BODYMORE MURDERLAND
By Delmont Player
FOR THE LOVE OF A BOSS
By C. D. Blue

BOOKS BY LDP'S CEO, CA$H

TRUST IN NO MAN

TRUST IN NO MAN 2

TRUST IN NO MAN 3

BONDED BY BLOOD

SHORTY GOT A THUG

THUGS CRY

THUGS CRY 2

THUGS CRY 3

TRUST NO BITCH

TRUST NO BITCH 2

TRUST NO BITCH 3

TIL MY CASKET DROPS

RESTRAINING ORDER

RESTRAINING ORDER 2

IN LOVE WITH A CONVICT

LIFE OF A HOOD STAR

Cum for Me 7